TO FIX A CURSE

TO FIX A CURSE

EFFIE ROSE

THORNGARDEN PRESS

For my mom, who taught me to fix toilets, tile floors, and read a novel in one day.

And for my dad, who took me to the hardware store on the weekends.

-ER

ONE

I stabbed the dirt with a screwdriver and another dandelion joined its wilting fellows in the wheelbarrow.

My phone rang.

Without even looking at the screen I told Grandma, "It's Dad."

Of course it was. He and my grandma were the only ones who actually called me. The rest of my friends texted, like normal people.

I tapped the screen. "Hello?"

"*Kassandra. Sorry to interrupt your less-than-leisurely vacation. You got a couple of minutes, kid?*"

"Sure." I wasn't sad at all to have a reason for a break. I clambered to my feet and made for the porch. "What's up?"

"*Good news and bad news. Pick one.*"

"Um, probably the good?"

Grandma unapologetically eavesdropped from the other side of the porch rail. She shot me a wry smile, which I returned while pulling my legs up to crisscrossed on the porch swing. "Okay, shoot."

"I bought us a project. A house!"

My heart jumped. We'd dreamt of turning over an old fixer-upper together for as long as I could remember.

"You're going to love it. It's in North Denver, and it's old. Really old. Victorian. Right up your alley, Kaz."

"Downtown?"

"Yep. You can transfer to Speer High. It's so close you can walk. I'll talk to Barry about getting you in for the fall."

Transfer? I sucked in a startled breath, but he kept talking. *Move?* I wasn't hearing him over the ringing that increased its volume in my ears and the scream that tried to climb out the back of my throat.

No high school junior wanted to be told she was moving—not when she'd made varsity volleyball. I blinked and gripped the seat of the swing. In no world would this ever be good news. "I can't move. Dad—no." My chest constricted, my neck hot despite the afternoon fog that blew fingers of cloud into the city. "I worked hard for an Advanced Placement schedule. What about volleyball? Dad, this is horrible timing. That's your *good* news?" My gut clenched with dread.

"Well, yeah. You're always talking about wanting to fix up one of those old places. I mean, I guess you don't have to change schools right away—you could commute."

As if my beat-up little 1980 pickup could handle that kind of demand. The line was silent for a moment. I'd not given him the reaction he'd expected.

"Look, it needs a ton of work, so that leads me to the bad news—I need you to come home early. We'll get all hands on deck and get this place renovated before school starts. I'm changing your return flight to have you come home on Friday."

I put two fingers to my forehead and stayed silent through only my stubborn act of will. I heard him tapping out his agitation with his pen on the table. I didn't know what to say.

"I know you and your grandma had a lot planned, but I need you here."

I still didn't say anything.

"Could you put your grandma on for a sec?"

Still speechless, I handed the phone off.

She pulled off her muddy gloves and placed them on the porch step. Frowning, as she did when interacting with technology, she held it to her ear. "Jim?"

I fidgeted with the chain on the porch swing while she listened.

"Okay, I'll have her call you back in a little bit." She studied the screen, probably trying to figure out how to hang up, but it went black on its own. She shrugged and placed it facedown on top of her gloves.

"Grandma, no!" I snatched it up and wiped a smear of dirt off the screen before sitting back in the swing, this time with my phone clutched in my lap.

I glanced apologetically at her. I hadn't meant to shout, but she didn't take very good care of electronics.

"I'm sorry, I forget how delicate those things evidently are." She pulled her gray braid to one shoulder and settled herself next to me on the swing.

We sat silently for a while, before she patted my knee. "Sounds like there's change on the horizon."

I scratched my thumbnail into the soft wood of the swing's armrest. "Yep."

"We've gotten a lot done already, and we still have enough time this week to finish painting inside. We've done good work."

My temper rose, and I didn't even try to restrain it from boiling over. "How can he do this to me? How can he just go out and buy a house while I'm away? I don't get any say in the matter? Doesn't he care how it affects me?" I ground a rose leaf into the porch deck with my sneaker, and the chlorophyll left a smear on the wood. "I just got here, and I never get to see you. And I'm supposed to just drop what I'm doing because he bought some dump, and he needs cheap labor?"

She drew her mouth into a sympathetic line and nodded, pulling me to her side.

She was strong and soft at the same time, and the most mom-ish thing I had. Instinctively I curled into her, inhaling the peppery floral and tea-tree scent that was so distinctly my grandma, and fought to hold the tears behind my lashes.

"I know, baby girl. I was looking forward to spending the summer with you." She smoothed my hair. "You could be doing something more fun than cleaning up an old lady's house, but I've enjoyed it."

"I know, right? We were going to refinish your bookshelves, and now there's no time. And we're moving? What am I going to tell Jenny?" I'd lived in the same house since I was born, my best friend in the house just ten feet from our dining room window. Quieter I said, "Why would he move us now?" I swatted a lock of hair away from my mouth and met Grandma's gaze, catching the pained expression.

I knew why, and she did too. It had been eight years, but it was June. Dad was always reckless in June—the anniversary of Mom's death. He couldn't think about anyone else right now.

I was so mad I could spit. "It's so selfish." I knew I was throwing a tantrum, but I couldn't stop. My throat hurt, and I was crying.

Grandma didn't defend her son. "It's going to be hard;

I'll grant you that. Your memories will follow, but I don't blame you for not wanting to leave." She was silent for a moment. "You've got the truck now, so that'll help you see your friends. Still, you've never been one for sudden changes. It's almost too much to take in at once."

I bit my lip. I couldn't even think. Mom. Jenny. No, I didn't want to think.

Tears blurred the hillside of rooftops and the distant Bay.

The breeze shifted, and the aroma of Grandma's incense wafted through the screen door, making San Francisco smell how outsiders expected San Francisco to smell.

"A lot is going to change." She patted my leg again. After a moment she ventured, "You know, though, change can be good."

I sighed. "Why do people only say that when something sucks?"

She chuckled. "Did I hear your dad say the house is old?"

I knew what she was doing and I didn't want to play. I was still mad. "It's Victorian."

"Mm, your favorite kind of house. It will have history." Her eyes, almost as dark as mine, crinkled in the corners. "Who knows what you'll find."

I stretched my legs out and rested them on the porch rail, then drew a slow, shaky breath. "Old houses *can* be pretty cool."

"I've always felt a connection to my old house. It has character. It's seen wars and recessions and the lives of at least half a dozen families." She touched the plank siding behind the swing. "My boy learned to walk right here on this porch. And later he knocked his head open on that step." She pointed with her chin. "In those days the doctor'd come to you. He stitched your dad up, right there in the front room."

I sniffed and wiped my face with the heel of my hand. "You're saying there's enough of our blood in the planks to make this house family?"

"Blood, sweat, and tears, baby girl. Your new place will be like that. A house with a soul." She sat back and frowned, and the swing stopped. "It sounds like your dad has taken on quite a project. I might just invite myself back with you. How about we spend the rest of the summer repairing an old house—just a different one than we'd planned? And, of course, I'll feed you home-baked pastries so you won't starve. If I know your dad at all, I can predict he'll get lost in the work and you two will eat nothing but delivery pizza unless I intervene."

I half-smiled, somewhat cheered. "That'd be great."

"Big changes. Say, that gives me a thought." She rose and disappeared through the front door.

I pulled the tiny brass gear out from my pocket and rolled it between my thumb and forefinger. I'd found it in the alley yesterday, shining brightly against the concrete, and I had no idea what it could have been from—only about a half inch across and a fat quarter inch deep—but its sharp little teeth felt good on my skin right now. And I did love brass.

When she emerged a moment later, she was holding a small velvet bag—her tarot deck. She handed it to me. "Shuffle them, please. Project your questions into the deck."

I groaned but took the cards, tucking the gear back into my pocket. "Grandma, you know I don't believe in this."

"Then do it for fun."

They were bigger than playing cards, harder to shuffle and soft from decades of use. The gray-flowered borders were frayed and torn. I turned them sideways and fanned their longest edges together—they fit in my hands better that way. I didn't have a question. I concentrated instead on the pastel artwork on the backs of the cards so I wouldn't focus on my anger and accidentally channel it into them.

Not that it was real anyway.

I cut the deck into three piles.

She took it from me and laid out the Celtic cross pattern on the seat cushion between us, leaned over the spread, and smiled. "That's my girl—the High Priestess. Intuition. This represents you."

"What—in the future?"

"Always. Your nature." She tapped a few other cards. "You drew the lovers." She glanced sidelong at me in a conspiratorial expression.

I laughed in spite of my bad mood. "See? That's what I'm talking about. Your cards are misinformed."

"Give them time. This deck sometimes gets the present and the future confused—though perhaps there's information you're withholding?"

"Gram—"

"I'm sorry. I won't tease."

"Clearly it's confused, and classifying any of my former interests as lovers would have been a bit euphemistic."

She turned another card. "The moon. Insecurity and anxiety. The Nine of Swords, more anxiety—nightmares."

That one grabbed my attention, and Grandma noticed.

"Are you having bad dreams?"

"Kind of. Sometimes."

She nodded. "Reversed Wheel of Fortune." She pursed her lips. "Bad luck. Loss of control."

"It's pretty clear I don't have a lot of say in what happens to me, so—" I shrugged. I wasn't paying a lot of attention anymore. My thoughts wandered back to the nightmare I'd had every night for a week. The abandoned street. The heavy clothes. The lightning.

How did it know? But then I reminded myself that it didn't know. It was wrong about the Lovers—the Nine of Swords was just a coincidence.

Grandma collected her cards and slipped them back into the velvet pouch. "What do you say we wrap it up out here and get an early dinner at the Wharf? Gardening is good for the soul, but melted butter is what's best for the taste buds. Do you want to call your dad back now, or send him a message that you'll do it later?"

"Later, I think." I flicked a piece of mulch off the armrest and exhaled. "I need time to think, but I do have questions." I needed to text Jenny first. She'd help me sort out my thoughts. She was going to be so mad.

"Sounds reasonable to me." She turned my chin so I looked her squarely in the eye. "You're just like your father."

"I've heard that before, and it doesn't always sound like a compliment."

"You know, adults aren't perfect, but most of us are doing the best we can. Sometimes kids pay the steeper price for our decisions. I'm sorry for that." Her dark eyes bore into mine. "Nevertheless...It's going to be fun, you know. This project."

I nodded and returned a small smile. "I hope so."

TWO

It was night, and I was in that place again. The one with the flickering yellow gas lamps and closed, empty storefronts.

I smoothed creases from the skirts of an old-fashioned, tight-bodiced dress and raised my chin in defiance of the chill on the night air.

There was no traffic on this well-lit city street. No cars, no carriages, no pedestrians. No shop owners. Not even a stray cat. And no sounds but the ones I made.

Like the world around me was on mute.

I walked out into the gravel street, crunching my way to the corner, and, of its own accord, my head turned toward the peak-roofed house on the right. I didn't know if I was intentionally homing in on it as my objective, or if I'd been drawn by its command—I never could tell, but I couldn't halt my progress if I tried.

And I'd tried.

The three-story Victorian on the corner was similar to the others up and down the street, and the street next to it, and the one after that. Except this one had an almost imperceptible incandescence in one of the upstairs windows.

I stopped once my shoes touched the sandstone walk.

It felt like the house itself was watching me. Seeing me. Taking my measure.

I crossed my arms, tried to breathe as deeply as the corset would allow, and counted to three. The light in the window went out.

Two seconds later a still-green maple leaf fluttered to the ground. I'd seen that leaf fall at least a dozen times.

One expected the experience to get old, but it was like flipping through a scrapbook of people or places I loved.

The house intimidated me, but I loved it.

I thought it loved me. It definitely knew I was here, and it leaned toward me in a beckoning posture.

I was afraid for it. Because at exactly the count of thirty-one, a bolt of lightning cut through the clear night sky.

Reaching for the house. Reaching for me.

And I couldn't move, so I stood, eyes wide, and watched it strike.

THREE

I took a deep breath, relished the lightness of Denver's thin air—the lightness of home—and ambled down the jetway to meet Dad in the main terminal. Grandma said she'd see us next week after she'd wrapped things up at home.

"Hey, Pops." My face smooshed against his chest when he squeezed me.

Dad was tall with thick, dark hair like mine, but his curled tightly around his head and across his short beard. Where I was built skinny like a sapling, he was a thick and sturdy oak.

"Hey, brat," he said in his deep Paul Bunyan voice. "Sorry to cut your trip short, but I'm glad to see you. I missed you."

"I missed you too," I admitted.

I collected my bags, and Dad held up the keys to his Subaru. "Want to drive?"

I hated the freeway. "Nah." I aimed for the passenger seat and, once we were rolling, asked again for the stats on the house.

"It was listed as a four bedroom, one-and-three-quarter bath," Dad said. "The main floor bedroom is set up as an office or library. The attic space is large and could be something someday. There's a basement, but it's just bare stone and junk."

I perked up. "Junk?" I envisioned trunks of old clothing and antique treasures. "You mean the house still has stuff in it?"

"Not really. Just a few bits of garbage no one ever threw in the bin. You can see for yourself." He held up a fat legal envelope. "We closed four hours ago."

It was a done deal.

I sat back in the seat and lapsed into my earlier funk. I really didn't appreciate being left out of such an important decision. I couldn't help but be a little miffed.

I said nothing else for the next twenty minutes.

He didn't seem to notice.

When Dad coasted to a stop in front of the chain-link construction fence, a wave of nausea swept over me and my stomach lurched. I grabbed at the handle above the door and slapped my other hand over my mouth. It wasn't like me to be carsick, but it took a moment for the world to steady and the scene to right itself.

Airplanes are cesspools, and now I'm coming down with the stomach flu. Perfect.

And just like that, the dizziness passed and I was fine again.

Peeking out from behind the overgrowth of trees on the broad corner lot was a dilapidated two-and-a-half story house. I immediately recognized the turn-of-the-century pitch of the roof, a ninety-degree angle at its apex, and my breath caught. It was beautiful. And by beautiful, I meant really ugly. A mess of decaying bad decisions on what had once been beautiful.

It needed me.

It was a classic old home, like the half-dozen other better-kept ones on the same street, like the one in my dream, even, but without the second-floor balcony and ornate brickwork.

"It's a handyman special, Kaz." Dad's eyes smiled even before his mouth did, and his enthusiasm was more than a little contagious. He pushed himself up and out of the driver's seat. "Welcome to our new home. Know a good handyman?"

"Nope." I climbed out and slammed the door. "You'll have to do." Immediately, I felt a twinge of guilt. I'd meant to joke and I thought that was how Dad took it, but it had come out kind of mean.

If the house had ever been pretty, a hundred years of abuse and bad design choices had hidden that. Still, it stood obstinately tall.

In the fading daylight, I could make out cracked mustard-yellow siding and plastic imitation stonework that clung to the exterior with little more than a prayer. The porch looked rotten and one support had failed. The south-east corner hung crookedly, pulling the façade into a lopsided frown. The grass and weeds sat shaded by gnarled fruit trees, one dripping bright-red cherries and guarded by a very busy raven. The yard looked as though it hadn't been tended in a decade.

"It's a dump," Dad admitted. "The land is worth more

than the house, so it was slated for demolition. I couldn't help myself."

"You're messing with me, right?" I laced my fingers through the fence while Dad worked a key into the padlock. The breeze whipped my hair across my face, so I dropped my hold on the wires and twisted my dark frizz into an elastic. "What is it, a 1900?"

Dad's little hobby of rescuing and restoring antique furniture translated, in my genetic code, to an obsession with turn-of-the-century antiques, particularly architecture and brass hardware.

"Nineteen oh-one," Dad answered and nodded his approval. "Good eye."

"So it's really Edwardian, not Victorian. I mean, Queen Victoria died in January 1901, so unless it was built at the very beginning of the year, I don't think it counts."

He fixed his gaze on me and raised an eyebrow. "Okay, one—you're a nerd. Two—I don't think real estate agents are so precise when writing their marketing blurbs."

"They should be."

He swung the gate all the way open. "I know you want to see it, but we'd better be quick. We're losing daylight and the electricity might not be back on yet." He handed me a headlamp. "They're supposed to take this construction fence away tomorrow. The place was owned by an investor. When the company went belly up, it sat vacant until they unloaded it. I had two hours to make the decision to bid on it."

"When do you expect we'll move?" I asked as my boots squished up the walk through several years' accumulation of leaves.

"Two months, maybe? It's tricky because we can't really pay for two mortgages and a renovation at the same time, so we kind of need to hustle. There's so much to do, and we'll do a lot of it ourselves. It's a little hard to put a firm date on it yet."

I grumbled.

"Look, you could start the year at your old school, if you want. You'll have to decide for yourself if you're going to transfer to the local high school when we sell the Littleton house. Fifteen miles is a pretty long commute when Speer's only seven blocks away."

I glanced at the painted-brick bungalow to the south and wondered who my new neighbors would be. The lights were on in one of the rooms, but I couldn't see anything through the mini blinds. They wouldn't be as cool as Jenny, that's for sure.

I clomped up onto the porch, but then, sensing the softness of the wood, stepped more gingerly and peered into the grimy window, cupping my hands around my face to reduce the glare. It was the living room.

Warm evening wind stirred the leaves and whipped loose hairs that caught in my mouth and lashes.

"She's back."

"Who is?" I asked my dad, dropping my hand from the pane.

"Hmm?" He was still fiddling with the multitude of door locks.

It hadn't been his voice I'd heard.

FOUR

My mouth went dry and I recoiled from the window like I'd been bitten. *What the hell was that?*

I turned on my heel, scanned the porch and yard but saw no one besides Dad. Backing away from the window I reached what was left of the railing, then edged over to the step, where I turned back to stare at the more-than-a-hundred-year-old glass pane that had spoken.

"You didn't hear that?"

"Hear what?" He pushed the door open and glanced toward me, but I shook my head and took another step backward and down one step. He flipped the keyring around between his fingers and looked me up and down. "What's the matter with you?"

There had to be someone in the house. Someone right on the other side of the window. "Dad, don't go in there."

Could I have imagined it?

Another gust of wind, this one cooler, played against the tiny goose-bump hairs on my arms. I shivered and steadied myself against the weathered curve of the railing, and the moment I touched it a calm heat stole up my arm and across my shoulders, as if the worn wood itself transmitted it—not stealing my memory of the voice, but my fear of it.

Can a house calm fear? Can a house talk?

I stepped backward down the last three steps, partly still shying away, but also to get a better look at the house's tall-gabled face. Grandma was probably right about one thing—it had history. Secrets. It was probably really cool inside. But there was something more—it felt good. Like to my fingertips. And there was something comforting about this yard, this street. Even in the expiring daylight, there was almost nothing scary about it at all.

Fear had been replaced with—affection.

"I love it," I blurted, my boots thudding back up the steps.

"Glad to hear it." He held the screen door open for me and mussed my hair. "You're not normal."

I stopped at the doorway to touch the carved trim work. "Yeah, but that's my inferior genetics and shoddy upbringing, you know."

S tepping across the threshold into the entry brought the goose-bumps back. It smelled like an old church. Like aged lath and plaster. Like a real home.

I tapped at the push-button switches on the wall, and they clicked into place, but nothing happened. Nope, the electricity wasn't on, and the shadows that lurked on the edges of our flashlight beams definitely upped the creepiness factor, but I was a big girl and I could handle it. I just kept saying that over and over as I shone my light about the room. *I'm a big girl. I'm not scared.*

We stood in a high-ceilinged foyer, a built-in wooden bench flanking the two walls to my right. A U-shaped staircase with dark, carved balustrade dominated the space, and directly ahead of the front door stood another five-panel oak door, closed.

To the left, the room opened to the atrocity intended to be a living room. It was walled with dark faux-wood trailer paneling and had an acoustic-tile dropped ceiling like the ones in my high school, except dirtier. The room smelled like stale cat piss, cigarette smoke, and another organic something I was probably better off not identifying.

I poked at a bowed section of paneling by a hall door, and a pin nail clattered down the wall to the carpet. "Yech," I said. "The years have not been kind to this room."

Our flashlight beams danced around the filthy avocado-colored shag carpet, stained with traffic patterns the color of motor oil.

"There's hardwood under those rugs," Dad said. "And we'll rip out the paneling."

"And the ceiling tiles?"

"Yeah, about those—" He reached up and slid one of the panels aside.

I moved in close beside him and directed my beam of light through the gap, then sucked in an audible breath.

The original ceiling was a swirl of ornate plaster decorated with red and orange flowers and gold ribbons. What's more, it was at least ten feet high—a full two feet above the panels.

"Why would somebody cover that? They preferred a small, ugly, industrial living room?"

"The sixties," he said by way of explanation. "I'm quite certain the only good thing to come from them was me."

"Dad, didn't the sixties produce the Beatles? I seriously

worry about your self-esteem sometimes." I pushed past him, bumping him on purpose with my shoulder. "I wish we could find some way to build up your self-confidence."

I wandered back through the dining room and into the enormous kitchen, which was also carpeted but with low-pile industrial remnants pieced together, the edges over-lapped. I peeled back one of the corners to reveal a patch of grubby linoleum.

How much 409 will it take to make this place habitable?

The only appliance was a refrigerator—in the other spaces were just gaping holes dotted with clumps of what were most likely rotten food particles and insect carcasses. *Yummy.*

I startled at my own reflection in the wavy glass of the pantry door. For a moment my messy bun looked like an old-fashioned pompadour. I peeled off my headlamp and held it to the side to cut the glare so I could peer into what I would never have expected to be a fully furnished room.

"Holy cats—an antique icebox! Dad, check this out."

I fumbled for the handle to get a closer look. The floor-to-ceiling shelving was loaded with Mason jars, tins, and sacks of burlap or cotton.

"Just a sec, kid." He was still in the living room.

The pantry door popped open with the smooching sound that old doors made when they wore twenty coats of gummed paint. I swung the door wide and stared into—

An empty room. The shelves were bare of all but dust.

WTF?

I backed up and closed the door, then aimed the beam again through the window and pressed my face to the glass.

Empty shelves.

No. I swear to God there was stuff. I couldn't make that up.

I spun and surveyed the kitchen behind me. The appliances were still missing. The cabinets, still grimy.

And Dad was in the doorway, looking at me like I'd lost my marbles. "What about an icebox?"

Tentatively, I reached again for the carved doorknob and turned it.

Yep, empty pantry.

I closed the door.

Touched the doorknob again.

Nothing.

I backed up and looked to Dad in confusion, even though he had no idea why. He was already crossing the room, ostensibly to see the thing I was excited about that *wasn't* in the pantry.

It's the dreams. I haven't slept enough, and this house reminds me of the gaslight one.

"Is there something wrong with that door?" Dad asked. He opened it himself and shone his light past me into the pantry. "Oh. I thought you were saying there was an icebox still in here. That would've been something." He pointed to the spot where I'd swear I'd seen it. "But, yeah, that's probably what this section of shelf had been cut out to accommodate."

"When I looked through the window—" I let my voice trail off. I didn't know what I thought I saw.

He waited expectantly for me to finish the sentence. When I didn't, he ruffled my hair, knocking my bun askew. "Come look at the office."

Dad led the way, but when he turned the corner I followed closely on his heels, hurrying away from the dark behind us in the kitchen.

The little hallway terminated at that swinging entry-hall door. Along the way we found a tiny bathroom—an afterthought in a place that likely had an outhouse when it was built—and a fairly large room with floor-to-ceiling built-in bookshelves. Under normal circumstances I would absolutely nerd out about an in-home library, but my nerves were a little jangled still.

Dad rested his hand on my shoulder in the dark room, and I nearly jumped out of my skin.

"You okay?" he asked when I spun around at him.

I glanced to the hall and back. "Yeah. I'm good."

He pointed to the far wall. "That door opens to 38th. It would be handy if you ran a business out of the house or something. Having a separate customer entrance, I mean."

I cocked my head and furrowed my brows. "You planning a career change? I didn't know there was a call for middle-school shop teachers who work from home."

He thunked me on the back of the head with a flick. "No, not for me, smart aleck. This is an investment. We fix this up and we can sell it as either a home or as commercial space. The location is great."

"Oh. We're not staying here either? I thought you only bought a house. I didn't know it came with a new, migratory lifestyle."

"This lifestyle could pay for your college."

I nodded once and the headlamp beam bounced.

My thumb trailed along the fluted carving between two bookcases. "I guess I just like the idea of having a home to come back to."

"Look, I'm not saying we're going to just fix it and flip it, but we should keep resale value in mind as we make decisions."

"As you make decisions," I said.

"Don't be like that, Kaz." He turned his back on me and walked out into the hallway, and I followed again, not really wanting to keep up, but definitely not wanting to be alone in this creepy house that was ruining the second half of my high school career.

Before the hall door swung shut behind me, I cast another wary glance toward the kitchen and shivered despite the stale heat.

We climbed the beautiful-and-only-a-little-broken staircase and poked around the second-floor rooms. It looked like one of the original bedrooms had been split in half to make the bathroom and an odd little closet with a two-burner stove, single-basin sink, and a really old four-foot-tall Admiral refrigerator—the kind with a locking-latch handle. It wasn't plugged in—the electricity wasn't on anyway.

"Oh, that's gonna be a HazMat situation," I said.

"Yeah, I wouldn't open that without a respirator and a bucket of bleach solution."

"It's kind of cool though."

"You like all old crap, regardless of whether or not it's *actually* cool. If that thing works at all it'll be an energy hog. It goes."

"Hey, you could put in a little door here and have the only master bedroom in the neighborhood with an *en-suite* kitchen."

"I'd wager there are more of these in the neighborhood than you think. Most of the big, old houses around here were divided up for apartments at one point or another."

"Sweet. We can move in, *and* I can have my own place?"

"That's my plan," he draped his arm across my shoulder. "Shouldn't be any reason for you to move out from under my watchful eye until you're at least thirty."

"That's not what I meant."

"Then you should have phrased it differently."

I hated when he won.

It was fully dark out, so the only light came from our headlamps, and the beams danced over everything we glanced at.

"What's this supposed to be?" I opened a door between the master bedroom and the stairway and found a small space—probably only six-by-eight—with bare wood floors and an aluminum, louvered window.

Dad stepped into the space and knocked on the wall. "I don't know. It looks like they just enclosed a porch. Maybe for another bedroom."

"That's a tiny bed—" A memory clicked into place, and I dropped my voice. "Wait, you mean there *was* a second-floor balcony? It didn't look like it from outside."

"It probably didn't because that beautiful harvest-gold siding conceals it. I think we should open it back up. I'd rather have another porch than a useless little room."

I murmured, "Yeah, sure." But my mind was on a darkened corner house with a balcony and a glow in the upstairs window.

I reached a tentative hand to the painted brick wall.

Warm. Like it was radiating back the heat of the day.

Warm. Like living flesh.

I jerked my hand back when the wall shivered. It couldn't have been the wall. My hand must have twitched and it just *felt* like it had been the wall.

"Good," Dad said. "See? We made a decision together."

I didn't reply.

I was inside *that* house.

Dad bought *that* house.

I drifted back into the hall and opened the door to what I expected to be a linen closet, but it was a narrow stairway.

Dad climbed the steps behind me, but he grabbed me

by the back of my shirt when I reached the landing. "Let's not walk on the damage until we can have it inspected, okay?" He nodded toward the black stains on the surface of the hardwood.

Roof leak.

I was appalled. "You haven't had it inspected?"

"Of course I had it inspected," he said, like I was the one being stupid. "But the house was listed as-is, and it was a steal either way. I'm bringing in a structural engineer to look into a few areas of concern, and this is one of them."

"What's this going to be?" I asked. The attic was a long open space with slanting gabled ceilings and only two windows, one at the front of the house, the other at the back.

"I don't know. Maybe we could frame it out for three or four more bedrooms, what with it being just the two of us. Sure would be nice if we had some more space or something."

"I know, right, Dad? We're going to rattle around in here. Why did you buy such a big house?"

"Because it was spectacular. And cheap. And I'd have been stupid not to. And if I hadn't, someone would have knocked it down."

I tapped my chin with my thumb. "You know, you could set up the first floor as commercial use with second and third floor living space. Like when people used to live above where they worked?"

Dad squeezed my shoulder then steered me back to the treacherous, steep stairs. "That's my little architect."

"Restoration contractor, Dad."

We descended back to the second floor, and then the first.

I passed my hand over the smooth banister on my way

back to the foyer. "I love this," I whispered. "Can we come back tomorrow? I want to check out the backyard and basement."

"We'll have to," Dad said. "The electricity should be on first thing. The roofers will be here at seven, and we're having the first roll-off delivered." He held open the heavy door for me to pass ahead of him into the night.

"What's a roll-off?"

He locked the house behind us. "Construction dumpster."

We headed for the car. I shoved my hand into my pocket and my fingers closed on the little brass gear instead of my lip balm. A warm breeze tickled my face, and I glanced back to the house.

Had it been my imagination, or had I just seen a pale golden light fade from the upstairs window?

Jenny was sitting with an impatient look about her in the glow of her front-porch light when we pulled into our drive. She hopped to her feet and jogged across the lawn, appearing at my door before I even unbuckled my seatbelt.

"Hi, Mr. West," she said.

"Hello, Jenny." Dad pocketed his keys. "You girls can have an hour, but it's already late. In by ten thirty, Kaz."

"'Kay, Dad."

Jenny's eyes were wide with the usual drama she was always in the middle of either experiencing or creating. "Omigod, what took you so long? I thought you said your flight came in at six-something."

"It did. We went to see the new house."

"Ugh. I can't even." She grabbed my wrist, pulled me out past the garage door and over to the flat-topped boulder that sat between our houses.

I climbed onto it and stretched my legs across the top of the stone. The smooth surface radiated warmth from the heat of the day, even though with the sun down the air was getting cool.

I unrolled my flannel shirtsleeves and scooted back to the edge of the rock.

Jenny didn't sit down. She stood behind me like usual and messed with my hair, which felt amazing, like when my mom used to arrange my French-braided pigtails in the mornings and brushed them out again in the evenings when I was little.

She tossed her own hair over her shoulder. "I've got news. News!" Both Jenny and I had dark hair halfway down our backs, but Jenny's had a healthy, glossy sheen and mine made waves and frizz.

I opened my mouth to reply, but she went on—her voice a stage whisper. "I got a job!"

"Wow. Congratulations. I didn't know you needed one. Um, tutoring?"

"Oh, I'll keep doing that." She parted my hair with an expertly enameled fingernail and twisted a section back. "It's actually my cover."

"Your—your what?" I raised my eyebrows and tried to look over my shoulder to communicate the expression, but she held a fat hank of hair tightly enough that I couldn't. "Why does this sound dodgy?"

She ignored the question. "Cheveaux salon, the one right next to the coffee shop where I tutor, needs a receptionist. My parents won't even know I'm not just collecting hours."

"Uh, you're not going to tell them?"

"No. God, no. The salon only needs me three nights a week. I'll be done by nine, so it's totally believable that I just took on another student or two. But here's the thing."

She passed a braided section over my shoulder. "Here, hold this."

I did, and she separated out another section.

"I can apprentice with them."

"What's that mean?"

"It means I'll be doing the actual job. Shampoos. Blowouts."

Ah, there it was. She wouldn't defy her parents just to stand behind the counter in a salon, but *doing hair* was too enticing an opportunity to pass up.

Jenny's dad expected her to become a doctor, like he was. He sent her to a private STEM school, and Jenny was freakishly book smart. She breezed through her classes, tutoring on the side to rack up community service hours for her résumé—and also because she liked telling other people what to do. But she had no intention of becoming a doctor, or even a teacher. She wanted to own a salon, and she only had two years to convince her parents to let her major in Business Management instead of Bio–PreMed.

"How's that work?" I asked.

"The apprenticeship?" She took the lock of hair from my hand and wound it around the other into what would likely be a very elaborate updo for a Friday night at home. "I'll work for them and take a summer course at the community college on Mondays."

"Jenny, you have to tell them. My dad had to sign all kinds of stuff for my dual-enrollment community college class, and you have to pay taxes on your income or whatever."

"I'll tell them," she insisted. "Just not yet. I need time to think of a way to convince them it's a good thing."

"What are you going to do when they find out and make you quit?"

She waved her fingers dismissively. "I dunno. I don't want to think about that right now."

"Okay."

We fell into silence for a moment. I wondered if she was sulking. She twisted the rest of my hair around the bun she'd made on top of my head.

I sighed contentedly.

"Got a pencil?" she asked.

"Yeah." I pulled two from my bag.

She took them both and slid them crosswise into the bun to secure it, then snapped a picture with her phone. She showed it to me. My hair looked even better than it felt when she did her magic.

When I handed the phone back to her, she'd already pulled the pencils back out and was finger-combing through it to start on the next style.

"What's the house like?" she asked.

"Old. And really, really big."

"Ooh. Is it spooky?"

I turned my head to look at her. "Oh, you don't even know."

I told her about how I heard someone talk and thought I saw stuff in the pantry that wasn't there.

"How many Red Bulls had you had?" She parted my hair down the center. "And where is this place?"

"West of Downtown, by Dad's school off Speer."

"Wait," she cut in and dropped the section of hair she was holding. She came around to stand in front of me. "Speer and what?"

"Um, Federal?"

A broad smile spread across her face. She threw her head back and snorted a half laugh.

"What?"

"Cheveaux is, like, blocks from there," she said. "Seriously, now I have every reason to hang out in that neighborhood."

I groaned. "Do NOT use me as a cover with your parents."

"No, Kaz, this is perfect. You may not be next door, but I'll be over there all the time!" She dropped her hold on my hair and climbed onto the rock next to me. "City boys. Downtown. Night clubs."

I was already shaking my head.

"You know you can't say *no* to me," she said. "Oh, we're going to get into so much trouble."

I rolled my eyes and pushed her off the rock. "That's what I'm afraid of."

It was dark.

I was in that place again. Almost.

Not across the street where all the stores were.

In the yard, right about where I stood when the lightning struck.

Instinctively I cowered, anticipating the flash and crack, but it didn't come. After a moment I relaxed. But only a little.

It was darker because the trees were in full leaf. They blocked the glow of the street lamps. What's more, there were no lights on in the house—my house—this time.

The hairs on the back of my neck prickled.

I was being watched.

I stepped into the shadows. That didn't ease the sensation, though I was surprised and pleased to have the freedom to direct my movements.

There was a stone bench to the right of the walk. I sat on it, hidden from all directions but from the house itself. Still, the feeling persisted.

I could only see a little section of street through the thick foliage.

Empty.

Eyeing the shadows of the porch and rosebushes, I found no one.

It was as though the house itself were watching me, so I turned my gaze to it—the two second-story windows, like eyes over the spindle-toothed smile of the porch.

As quickly as it came the sensation was gone, the absence making me all the more certain of its existence in the first place.

Then—a vibration. A creak, low groan, and the scraping rumble of thousands of bricks moving against one another.

Now I was frozen. I couldn't move, couldn't run for safety, couldn't budge from the bench. I squeezed my eyes closed and braced for the inevitable—the house was going to fall.

But it didn't crumble.

The creaking tapered to an end, and I dared a peek. Mortar dust wafted on the evening air. But every brick remained in place.

The house stood taller. It no longer appeared slumped and derelict, but reached proudly and defiantly into the night sky.

And this time, when the tiny bumps rose again on my flesh, I was certain. The house was watching me.

Every fiber of my being thrummed with certainty that it had recognized me.

We sat in acute awareness of each other.

And we were both waiting.

The edges of my vision blurred before I found out what we were waiting for.

The next day Dad and I arrived early in our demolition finery. Our jeans and long sleeves felt good against the morning chill, but we'd roast in them later.

"I don't suppose this place has air conditioning," I commented.

Dad rumbled his laugh. "Sorry, kid. I'm going to install a swamp cooler ASAP—probably day after tomorrow. Work hard in the morning—rest in the afternoon."

Two of Dad's coworkers met us to help with the heavy lifting. Both were teachers from his school—guys I've known since I was a baby. They were like uncles to me. Uncles who corrected my grammar and quizzed me on Civil War trivia.

Armed with respirators, safety goggles, leather gloves, and crow bars, we stomped into the front room like a troop of redneck *Star Wars* LARPers. Since it was a fairly easy job, I got to work pulling down the ceiling panels and the aluminum grids on which they sat, revealing the gorgeous but neglected plasterwork. Dad used a crowbar to yank off sections of wall paneling, while Mr. Daniels and Mr. Lowmaster pulled out all the carpet from the house, starting with the kitchen.

"Holy hell!" Dad exclaimed and pulled down a panel sheet in the corner of the dining room. "There's a built-in back here."

Sure enough, the fascia had been built out to completely conceal a carved shallow sideboard and hutch.

I dropped my tools and edged in next to him as he swiped a gloved hand across the wood. "Mahogany," he said.

The mirror was speckled where the silvering layer on the back had deteriorated and yellowed, but the effect was beautifully antique. I stepped closer, and my reflection moved into view.

At once my stomach lurched, and the image in the mirror spun. I caught a glimpse of the flowered ceiling as it swam by. And the fireplace—*a fireplace?*

I staggered and threw my hand out toward the countertop to balance myself, pulling off my mask and covering my mouth with my other hand.

Don't vomit.

Dad grabbed my elbow and steadied me. "Are you all right?"

In the mirror now, I saw the ornate ceiling, the piles of rubbish on the hideous carpet, and two walls, still covered in paneling.

"It's your respirator," Dad said. "It's hard to breathe in those sometimes, especially when it gets hot." He pushed me toward the entry, his hands firm on my shoulders. "Go outside and take in some fresh air for a spell," he ordered.

But it wasn't hot yet—it was only about eight a.m. Still, I did as I was told. I picked my way past the rubble and hazarded a glance at the room's southern wall. It had a built-out section too.

"There's a fireplace behind that." I pointed with my leather glove.

"You may be right." He appraised the wall. "Now get outside and get some water in you."

Obediently, I headed out.

But that respirator'd had nothing to do with my dizzy spell, because I hadn't been wearing it last night when the pantry door had tripped me out.

I moved gingerly across the rotten porch and down the steps. Standing on several years' accumulation of leaf litter and mud, I whirled about and stared at the face of the house in broad daylight.

The houses were closer together than they'd been in my dream. One was built just feet away from the south wall of our house. They must have subdivided the property and sold off the extra lots. The front door was plain, not leaded glass and oak—it had been replaced. But the shape of the house—and if that wall there were just a railing—

Under that siding was brick, and probably the scalloped-shingled gables and woodwork I'd seen so many times in my dreams. This was most definitely that house. And it was messing with my head.

Last night I'd stood in this spot while the house shook.

There had been an apple tree. Where was the apple tree? The bench? Gone.

I backed down the walk to the curb, still staring at the front of the house, then crossed the weed-possessed tree strip and wandered onto Grove Street, which, like in my dream, was untrafficked. This time, though, a half-dozen parked cars occupied the perimeter of the asphalt, and vehicles sped by on 38th. *The shopping district.*

I pivoted and stared at the house that would be our home someday and said aloud, "Why have I been dreaming about you all summer?"

A woman's haggard voice startled me. "*La vida es un sueño del que se despierta al morir.*"

I pivoted and stared at the bent old woman just a few feet away, a crocheted shawl draped across her hair. She carried a Save A Lot bag in one hand and leaned on a cane with the other.

Where had she come from?

"I'm sorry?" I said. "Uh, *no hablo mucho español.*"

She coughed into her shawl and repeated, slower this time and louder. "*La vida— es un sueño— del que se despierta — al morir.*" She patted my arm.

I shook my head. It was still as clear as mud. *The life, wha?*

She chuckled, and when she peered up at me she sucked in the corners of her mouth. "*Tienes los ojos.*" She brushed around me and waddled away along the sidewalk.

"I have the eyes?"

But she didn't look back. She probably hadn't even heard me.

I tapped a search into my phone.

Life is a dream you wake up from when you die.

"This place is nucking futs," I muttered under my breath, shooting the house an accusatory glance. As I walked back to its entrance I tallied the events, counting on my fingers with taps to my denim-covered thigh. The voice, the pantry, the dining room, the old lady. Oh, and the dreams. How many ticks did that count as, if I'd had at least two dozen of them?

I grabbed a water bottle from the car and carried it up to the porch. At the last second, I changed my mind and swerved out into the lawn, ducking under the branches of the cherry tree. The raven was gone. His loss.

I settled myself with my back to the tree trunk, elbows draped over my propped knees and took a swig from my water bottle. I plucked a pair of dark cherries from a low-hanging branch and popped them into my mouth.

They were sweet and perfect. Too delicious to let go to waste. I stripped a few more and rolled them around in my fingers while I thought.

That old woman was almost as creepy as seeing and hearing things that weren't there.

I didn't bother to play the "it's my imagination" game. I was past that. I'd dreamt about this house before I'd seen it. And I'd seen things that weren't there. Twice.

"There's no such thing as ghosts," I said aloud.

I frowned. *Who said anything about ghosts?* "There's no such thing as a haunted house, either."

I didn't really believe myself.

I spat out a cherry pit and took another long pull from my water bottle.

My gaze drifted to the south wall, where a chimney climbed the side of the house and pushed into the sky.

"See? That's what I'm talking about," I said aloud. "I knew there was a damned fireplace there."

EIGHT

Before entering the house, I pulled my respirator back over my face and ran smack into Dad, who was on his way out to check on me.

"Whoa, kid. You ready to get back to work?"

"Yeah."

"You sure?"

"Definitely." I added with certainty, "There's nothing wrong with me."

We clomped back into the living room to clear the debris, and he gestured to the far wall. "You were right," he said. "Fireplace."

"Yep," I said. It was just a tile frame, a board screwed over the opening to cut the draft, but it was a fireplace. "We should build a mantel. Put candlesticks on it, and hang a mirror."

The way it used to look.

"Sure," he replied, picking up his end of a stack of panels. He walked backward, letting me have the easier job. "If we wind up with a down day, we can let ourselves into the school and use the machines there."

We heaved the mess into the dumpster. "Is this house in your school's boundaries?"

"Yup," he replied.

"A really short commute then."

"It's a bit of a hike, but not a bad bike ride," he said.

"Won't it be weird, though? Running into your students all the time, like at the grocery store or the library?"

He snorted a laugh. "If I run into them at a library I'll give them extra credit. But, no. I mean, maybe sometimes. Still, I've often kind of wished I lived in the community where I work. I feel like such an outsider to my students sometimes, you know?"

Two hours later the guys had hauled out the debris, rolled and chucked the carpet, and Dad and I stood between the living and dining rooms admiring our work.

The ceiling plaster and walls wanted patching; the hardwood was discolored. Everything was dingy, but the rooms already seemed bigger and brighter.

"It's a shame the wallpapers are too damaged to restore, but maybe we can take pictures and replace them with something similar." I ran my hand along the seam in the dining room's blue stripes.

"You want to go through the work of ripping down wallpaper just to put up more wallpaper?" Dad asked.

"I don't know. It seems right for a hundred-year-old house to have wallpaper. The rooms upstairs have paint right over it. You can see where the strips overlap."

"We might have to deal with that at some point," Dad said. "Moisture in the paint can seep through the paper and make it lift and bubble. We'll add it to the list of projects for you to finish when I'm dead and gone and you inherit the house. Keep that in mind if you're ever tempted to cut corners and do shoddy work, kid. Don't pick your own pocket."

"I thought you said it was just an investment. Besides, when have you ever known me to do crap work?"

"Never," he admitted. "That's why I'm certain you aren't really my daughter. Must've been the mailman."

"A completely reasonable assumption, since I don't look a thing like you." I rolled my eyes.

"You sure look like your mom sometimes too, though," he said quietly. He was staring at his utility knife and clicking it open and closed.

Neither of us spoke for a minute.

I cocked my head, then threaded my arm around his waist.

He squeezed me into a can't-breathe bear hug.

"What would she think about the house?" I asked into his shirt.

"She'd hate it," he said and laughed, releasing me. "I mean, she'd be pleased that we're happy and busy, but she'd rather've left the construction to me while she tended the garden."

"We should plant a vegetable patch in her honor," I said.

"Okay. But maybe not today. Let's take a well-deserved break," he said.

"Lunch? I'm starving."

"My thoughts exactly." He shouted up the stairs, "Guys, wash up. We're eating!"

We scrubbed the dirt from our fingernails and faces, then stumbled through the mudroom and out the back door onto the patio. Someone, decades before, had laid red flagstone over the nearest quarter of the backyard. Trees and time had heaved some of them up, so the surface wasn't flat, but the potential was there.

"Holy partio, Batman," I said, taking in the riot of roses, irises, and grape hyacinth. A brick two-carriage garage squatted in the back corner of the yard, untended grapevines claiming almost its entire back wall. This backyard, left to its own devices, had turned itself into the Garden of Eden.

"Only adult-supervised parties on my patio, little one," Dad warned and hoisted our jug of lemonade from the cooler.

I smirked. "No, I was thinking of when you're dead and gone and I've inherited this amazing party yard."

"I'm going to live forever just to keep that from happening."

Mr. Lowmaster and Mr. Daniels joined us and helped set lunch on the ornamental concrete picnic table in the shade of an enormous cottonwood tree.

We chattered about construction timelines for the next half hour while filling our bellies, a pleasant distraction from the soreness of our muscles.

For the briefest of moments I was tempted to tell Dad about the mirror and the voice I heard, but then I didn't. After Mom passed he got weird—talked a lot about angels and the supernatural, and he got really overprotective of me. He was almost normal now, eight years later.

And I liked to keep it that way.

But I'd finished inhaling food and I was getting impatient, and he was only just now unwrapping his second sandwich, yakking with the guys.

"I'm gonna go poke around a bit." I wadded up my napkin and tucked it in the grocery sack we were using for trash.

"'Kay, kid, be careful," Dad said.

"Who do you think you're talking to?" I yanked his hat from his head and stuck it back on—backwards.

"You let A.J. work in there unsupervised. Kaz is way more responsible," Mr. Daniels said.

"*You* were supposed to be keeping an eye on him." To me, Dad said, "Forgive me. I was dadding. Can't be helped."

"'Sokay." I wandered through the back door and laundry room and into the grungy kitchen. Without the carpets it was a little less gross. Turquoise-and-white checkered linoleum squares could have been pretty, if not for pitting and damage and black spots of exposed adhesive where they were missing entirely.

I crossed the room to the pantry and peered through the window again, searching the empty shelves for signs of what I thought I'd seen last night. I grabbed the folding step stool from the corner and searched each shelf but found nothing.

Sighing, I returned the small ladder to its corner.

In the dining area I rested my palms on the narrow sideboard and gazed again into the mirror. A reverse image of the newly exposed living room walls reflected back at me. I stared into it, willing it to turn and spin the way it did this morning, but nothing happened. I pushed away with a huff of indignation. Basement "junk" called.

The narrow door from the mudroom to the cellar revealed steep three-foot-wide stair planks that were more akin to fat ladder rungs than actual stair treads.

The basement ceiling was low, less than a foot above my head. Dad would have to crouch. A dangling string turned on a dim incandescent bulb, illuminating the center of the room but not doing much for the rest of the space. A little bit of light filtered through two dirty windows.

The floor was cement, but not flat—like someone mixed up buckets of Quikrete, poured them out, and left gravity to do the smoothing, which was probably exactly what happened.

There *was* junk down here. Odds and ends. Dad was right—none of it looked very compelling. It was mostly garbage that never got carried out to the dumpster, probably because the stairway was too steep to negotiate.

But I did notice two little treasures hiding in the far corner of the space. One was a free-standing iron fireplace, and it looked like it was piped into the old kitchen chimney. The other was a vintage gas range from the fifties. Eight burners. Four oven doors. The thing had to be almost four feet wide.

It was going back into the kitchen, that was for sure.

I switched off the light and climbed the stairway, and then wandered up to the second floor to pick a bedroom.

The front room was the largest—Dad's claim. It had the house's two front-facing windows, the walls a pale yellow and the woodwork still the original dark, golden brown. The closet was surprisingly large—probably a third the size of the bedroom.

The back two bedrooms were equal in size. The one to the left was mint green and had just one window overlooking the backyard, where I saw Dad and Mr. Lowmaster clearing the patio table. The closet was pathetically small— only about two feet deep and with hooks instead of a clothing rod.

Oh, that'll need to be reconfigured.

The other bedroom was lilac and all the millwork was off-white. The two windows overlooked the backyard to the west and 38th to the north. I tugged open the closet door.

Jackpot.

This one was decent, maybe four-by-five. It, too, had clothing hooks along the wall, and also a shower-curtain tension rod, which couldn't possibly handle the weight of more than a handful of clothing hangers. Not even with that wire reinforcing it to the doorway molding.

I rolled my eyes. Crappy DIY.

Backing out and standing in the middle of the room, I turned slowly, taking it in.

This was my room.

I breathed in deeply and exhaled, smelling the plaster, wood, and age. It would smell of paint soon enough, but that antique house smell would come back, mixing with the scents of my lotions and laundry detergent. My idea of home was going to smell just. like. this.

The floor was wood, of course, and it was painted dark brown, but only around the outer two feet or so.

Those Edwardians. Painting hardwood. *Sheesh.*

I plopped my backside into the northwest corner of the room and tried to envision where my stuff would go. It was probably only a little over twelve-by-twelve, but the ceilings were at least nine feet high with a crown molding around the top and, thankfully, no popcorn texture. How this house survived the seventies without popcorn ceilings was a miracle, especially considering the atrocities of design in evidence downstairs.

"My Ikea bed is going to look stupid in here," I said aloud.

"You'll have to get a new one." Dad's voice boomed from the hall. His scruffy face appeared in the doorway. "Stake your claim?" he asked.

I nodded my head once. "This one has the second-best closet on the floor. I figure you'll want the other, since you think paying the bills earns you prime real estate."

He shrugged, indicating the indisputability of the jest. "Yep. You know, about that bed..." He shuffled over and planted himself next to me on the floor, a mountain of a man, even when seated. "I'll bet you could find a nice brass antique one. That'd look about right in here."

I leaned on his flannel-covered shoulder and considered it. A brass bed under that window, a fresh coat of paint, hardwood, maybe a fuzzy rug. "Yeah," I said slowly. "That'd be perfect."

"You could unload your desk too."

"No, the half spool stays. It's classy."

He rolled his eyes. "No, it's not. We need our money for contractors, but it's in the budget for us to get some new furnishings. I want you to make this house ours, you know?"

"C'mon, Dad, you know I'm going to get someone's trash and fix it up. It's what I do."

He cast me a sidelong glance and crooked smile. "And where'd you come by a habit like that?" he asked, gesturing at the room, the house.

"It's what I've heard said about apples and trees."

Dad slapped my back, pushing me to my feet—his nonverbal order to get back to work.

Clouds rolled in, and afternoon rain made the house almost a comfortable temperature, so we kept at it past our scheduled quitting time. By five o'clock I'd scrubbed and disinfected all the surfaces of the main and second floors. Even with protective knee pads and cleaning gloves, my limbs were sore and raw. But everything gleamed, thanks to the cleaning magic of blue dishsoap.

"I'm not sorry to be done with the bug carcasses," I said when Dad appeared in the doorway. "The grime is gone.

Anything that appears now is construction dust, and that's not nearly so nasty."

"Glad you said that, kiddo. I was just about to head over to Home Depot to pick up the sander so we can get started on the floors toni—" Dad ducked when my yellow rubber gloves soared past his face. "What?"

"No!" I said. "We're done."

"I was kidding!" He choked down a laugh and draped his arm across my shoulders. "We do need to plan out the next couple of days, but we can do that over a pizza and Cokes. Let's motor."

NINE

ad was busy with contractors and errands the next morning, so I dragged Jenny over to the house with me. Since we had the day to kill, I thought we'd go ahead and paint my bedroom. First, I gave her a quick tour.

Surveying the living room, Jenny nodded. "It's totally not my thing, but, yeah, I can see how it's totally yours."

"Totally?" I leaned with my elbow on her shoulder, since she was so much shorter than I was.

"Totally," she replied.

"The eighties called, and, like, they want their *totally* back," I said in my best Valley-girl accent.

"You really shouldn't point out other people's overuse of the outdated," she retorted. "I've seen your grunge-chic wardrobe and nineties-alternative music collection. You own more flannel than L.L. Bean. Your beloved *new* house—did it predate indoor plumbing and electricity?"

"Yeah. Probably."

We hopped back into my beat-up little green truck—a 1980 Plymouth Arrow—and puttered the couple of blocks over to the hardware store to pore over paint samples. I selected a flat white paint to coat the house's nicotine-tinged ceilings.

"If your ceilings are bright white, then you should have white trim too," Jenny insisted. "Unless you do a color."

"I know what you're trying to say—you don't think white and off-white go together, but I think bright white will be too modern looking. Totally incongruous."

"Totally?" She raised a penciled brow.

I snorted, grabbed a sample and plunked it down on the counter. "This one. Antique white. It's still white, just not 'hallelujah white.'"

She furrowed her brow in annoyed acceptance, snatched it up, and held it against the board of samples. "Okay, but use a purple like this," she said, pulling down a grayed lavender. "It's more on trend than the old-lady lilac that's in there now."

I held the samples together. "This is perfect. Nice pick." And it really was. I wasn't just appeasing her after not taking her advice on the trim.

She seemed placated.

While a gentleman mixed the paint, I noticed a gallon of dove gray on the mismatched paint shelf and grabbed it for the spare room. Dad hadn't shared any particular plans for the space, but I didn't think he'd object to Jenny and me taking paint off the list—and at three dollars, it would have been stupid to pass it up.

I paid with my dad's credit card, and the bored, middle-aged woman at the register didn't ask me to prove I was James L. West. She didn't bother to read the card, nor compare the signatures, which I just signed with my own name anyway.

As we gathered our haul, a boy about my age emerged from the back room donning his Clark's Hardware apron. Shiny, dark hair fell across his forehead, and, with his head down, I couldn't see his face. What I could see were square shoulders and the torso of a T-shirt model. He was not tall—probably five foot eight—but he was definitely all right to look at.

I closed my mouth, which had fallen open, and averted my gaze so he didn't catch me checking him out, but sensed that I had been a moment too late. My scalp prickled under the brush of his gaze.

When I glanced up again, he was looking right at me. He smiled.

My face got hot, the tide washing from my cheeks to my chin.

His smile deepened, eyes crinkling in amusement.

"Time to go," I said to no one and everyone, grabbed the receipt and hurried out the door.

I hadn't just asked Jenny over for the day because she was my best friend and I needed chat time—I asked her because she had mad skills with a paintbrush. With her precision, we didn't even need masking tape, which saved us a ton of time.

As she cut in with a brush and I rolled a fresh white coat onto the ceiling, she resumed her chatter. I wasn't listening very carefully because I was trying to make sense of the last few days. Eventually I interrupted when she paused for an opportune moment.

"I don't mean to sound like I don't care about your new job, but I need to hijack this conversation for a minute to talk about me."

Her false lashes blinked in surprise. "Omigod, I'm so sorry. I always do that."

"No, you don't," I lied. "I'm just going to butt in because I have to talk to you about this—it's making me crazy. You know how I thought I heard someone when I was looking through the front window?" I told her about yesterday's dizziness and the old-fashioned parlour I saw in the dining room mirror, and how an old lady talked to me in Spanish.

"Okay, so let me get this straight—you're having hallucinations. You dreamt about the house, and now your dad owns it. You saw groceries in the pantry and a restored living room? So you're seeing the future?" Her paintbrush hand hung loosely at her side, but the thumb of her other hand tapped the top of the ladder thoughtfully.

I shook my head. "No, it's not the future. In my dreams, the streets are still gravel, and the lights aren't electric. Everything in the pantry was weird—not packaged and labeled like normal food. I only saw it for a second, but I'm pretty sure it was old."

"So, it's the past?"

"Yeah."

"You think the house is giving you visions from its past, and what it has to show you are groceries and architecture?"

It sounded stupid, even to me, but I didn't have anything else.

"Something like that." I busied myself with the roller.

Jenny didn't move, and when I dared a glance at her she had her head tilted and one side of her mouth tightened in thought. Now it was her paintbrush hand that was tapping, flicking purple splotches onto her thigh.

"Look," she said apologetically, "I'm not saying it's not weird, I'm just saying it doesn't make sense."

"I know. It doesn't make sense to me either."

"I want to see."

"What, the old stuff?"

"Yeah, of course."

"It doesn't work like that, Jen. I've tried to make it happen again. It doesn't."

"Show me anyway."

We climbed down from our ladders, and I took her through the downstairs for the second time. Nothing seemed out of the ordinary, but Jenny was patient with me while I gushed about the hidden sideboard.

"I mean, look at this." I tugged open the top drawer. "It needs oil, but the mahogany is gorgeous. Look at those dovetails—they're perfectly smooth."

"Uh huh, yeah. Wood. They're made of wood. Exceptionally amazing wood," she said. "Are they all empty?" She tugged open the bottom drawer, and it was so short that it came out in her hands.

"Try not to break the house, Jenny. We just got it."

She shot me a withering glance and squatted down to line up the drawer with its guides.

A ripped remnant of wallpaper sat on the floor inside the drawer cavity. "Hang on, let me pull that out of there first."

And under the paper were two yellowed rectangles.

"What're those?" Jenny asked.

I turned them over in my hands.

One was a class picture. The typed title read "Saint Xavier School, Class of 1911." The other was a portrait of a handsome, dark-skinned young man.

"Oh, that is so cool," Jenny said. "Look at how old they look. I mean, if that's a senior picture they're only a year older than we are, but each and every person in that photo could pass for twenty-one today."

"It says 1911, Jenny. They're dead today."

"You know what I mean." She tilted my hand so she could get a better look. "That's the same guy—that one right there."

She was right.

I held the photos side-by-side. The guy from the portrait stood, wearing the same suit, in the second row of the class photo with eleven of his classmates.

"He's not bad." Jenny said.

"He's, like, a hundred twenty-seven."

"Well, he used to be good looking then. And don't try to tell me he's not your type. He's made-to-order yummy."

I had to agree. Dark hair slicked back. Eyes like coals, with a sleepy look, as though weighed down by his thick black eyelashes. I flipped both photos over, searching for a name, but their backs were blank.

"You should frame them and display them in the house. D'ya think?" Jenny said.

"I should look up St. Xavier yearbooks and see if I can get a name. It'd be cool to know more about who used to live here."

I handed them to Jenny, who set them on the narrow shelf.

"Come on. I kind of wanted to do two rooms today. Let's get back to it."

. . .

We didn't break for lunch until mid-afternoon, after we'd depleted our supply of Cheez-Its and Mountain Dew.

Jenny and I wandered back over to 38th, intending to seek sustenance at a nearby burger spot, but decided on a little taqueria with a sidewalk patio instead. While we munched on house-made tortilla chips and wicked good salsa verde, Jenny filled me in on more details of the salon job.

"Yeah, so I start tomorrow afternoon. I'm so psyched. They don't have a dress code *per se*, but they told me to dress 'fashion forward.' "

"That's not going to be a problem," I said. Even today—to paint—she was wearing short cutoffs, a sheer off-the-shoulder embellished tee over a black cami, and gray Vans. She looked like Hollywood. In spite of her recklessness with the brush, her clothes were pristine. Only her leg bore a streak of white and some purple freckles, but she made them look badass.

I, on the other hand, looked pretty bedraggled in jersey shorts and an old Nike tee from eighth grade volleyball camp, flannel shirt tied around my waist. Pretty rough, minus the pretty.

"Okay, don't look now. Hottiefest at two o'clock."

I immediately turned and looked straight into the gaze of Hardware Store Boy, who was waiting across the street for the signal to change. He held his skateboard by its trucks, same as the other two guys he was with.

He half smiled in our direction and nodded with his chin before he turned and said something to his friends. My cheeks flamed.

"I said, 'Don't look,' " Jenny muttered into her straw.

I didn't need to look over my shoulder again to know the light had changed and they were approaching. Skateboard wheels clicked loudly at each sidewalk crack, and boys were not particularly quiet in their natural habitat.

I was suddenly very interested in the salsa bowl.

The skateboards stopped. "*Hola, güeritas,*" a male voice said.

All three boys stood on the sidewalk, just a couple feet from where I was seated. The tallest, the one who'd spoken, leaned against the café rail, smiling a very flirtatious smile. At Jenny.

"*Buenas tardes. ¿Podemos ayudarle?*" she responded smoothly.

"*Ay, la china habla español,*" the tall one said to the other two.

Hardware Store Boy smiled at me. His other friend, a sturdy guy built like a refrigerator, avoided eye contact and looked like he was trying to blend in with a tree. He seemed nervous in the presence of the opposite sex, which I could totally sympathize with. His friend, though, appeared to have more than enough confidence.

"I am *not* Chinese," Jenny snapped. "I'm Korean."

"Nice to meet you, Korean. You're beautiful," Tall Boy said, his voice purring with Spanish inflection.

"No. My name is Jenny," she clarified, as though his mistake had been an honest one. "And thank you."

"Nice to meet you, Jenny. I'm Javier. *Estos son mis amigos Tito y Miguel.* They aren't as charming as I am."

Jenny asked, "But are they as modest?"

"Who could be?" Hardware Store Boy answered. He extended his hand for Jenny to shake, like it was perfectly normal for people our age to greet each other with handshakes. "Hi, Jenny."

Jenny seemed unfazed, shook his hand like she was an attorney or something, but I caught the amused sidelong glance she cast my way.

Hardware Store Boy turned to me with the same greeting.

Heat flared across my cheekbones, but I forced myself to meet his gaze. My hand touched his, and bright white light momentarily blinded me, like a camera's flash in a dark room, leaving in its wake wavy peripheral vision. His hand was warm, just a little rough, and still touching mine.

"I'm Miguel. And you are?" His eyebrows raised, and that thousand-watt smile never left his face.

"Kassandra—Kaz," I said, returning his smile and sitting up straighter to mimic Jenny's confidence. I tried to blink away the spots on the edge of my vision, while trying not to look like an idiot.

"It is truly a pleasure to make your acquaintance, Kassandra." He released my hand.

No one talked like that. He had zero accent—like a newscaster—but he was way too formal. The theater type, maybe.

"Thank you," I said automatically.

Javier vaulted over the patio rail and seated himself at the table next to ours, sliding his chair closer to Jenny's and facing her. "Did you order the tamales? Everyone orders the smothered burrito, but you should always get the tamales."

His friends went around through the gate, leaving their skateboards and his next to a giant potted plant before sliding into the other seats at his table.

"We got quesadillas," Jenny answered for us.

"Rookies," Javier admonished, shaking his head. He grabbed a tortilla chip from our basket and popped it in his mouth.

The plump woman from inside emerged with our order. After setting the fiery plates in front of us, she smacked Javier on the head with her towel. "Let my guests eat in peace. And don't sit there like a customer. *Si quieres comer, vete por tu comida.*"

"*¡Ay, Mami!*" Javier said, rising and protecting his face against another onslaught from her dishtowel. He disappeared through the front door.

She turned to Miguel and Tito and smiled sweetly to them.

Miguel was already standing, presumably to follow Javier.

The woman grasped his arms as he moved past. "How is your madre, *mijo*? And *abuelita*? You let me know if you need anything, okay? I send tamales home with you for tomorrow. You give them to Marta."

"Thank you, Señora Guzmán," he said, and kissed her on the cheek. "Oh, that reminds me. 'Uela had some oils for me to bring to you, but I forgot them on the kitchen table. I'll bring them after dinner."

"Bless you, child." She touched his forehead with her finger. "There's some horchata in the cooler. Go get some for yourself and Tito. Such good boys."

Miguel disappeared through the same door Javier did, and Tito moved to go help, or to escape, but Señora Guzmán stopped him.

"*Siéntate, Tito. Hay demasiados cocineros en la cocina.*"

She turned her attentions back to us. "How do you like it? Is okay?" Her English was heavily accented, and her smile was warm.

"It's delicious, Ma'am," I said.

"Now tell me the truth, was my son bothering you?" she asked, the question directed at me.

"No," I replied with complete honesty. He wasn't bothering me. He was bothering Jenny.

"This salsa is excellent, Señora Guzmán," Jenny said.

"Then come back every day," she replied and waved her dishtowel in the air before returning inside.

Tito was still seated at the table next to us, and no one seemed to know what to say. He looked really uncomfortable.

"C'mere, Tito," I said, not wanting him to feel left out. He was shy enough to make *me* feel like the extrovert. "Slide over and help us eat these chips."

His thick eyebrows knit together over his round face. "You sure?" he asked. His accent was very strong.

"Of course. We can't eat all this."

He moved into the chair Miguel had vacated and helped himself.

Jenny clapped her hands. "HiTea & Bean! You work there."

Tito cocked his head in surprise. "Yes."

"I was trying to figure out why you look familiar to me."

"You teach math, yes?"

"Yeah, I tutor."

He nodded. "You ever teach English?"

"I could." Something flashed in her expression, and they leaned a little closer to each other.

My gaze volleyed between them. Javier might be out of luck—looked like Jenny liked the quiet fixer-upper.

And just like that, they'd exchanged numbers. Javier didn't even know he'd been cast aside.

We lapsed into silence again, and I felt compelled to fill it to avoid the I'm-trying-not-to-look-like-I'm-trying-not-to-stare-into-your-eyes thing that was going on. "So what's your story, Tito? Are you from around here?"

He gave me a look. Obviously he was not. "I am from Mexico."

"That's cool. Where?"

"Chihuahua." He spoke in barely more than a whisper.

"Oh. The city of Chihuahua? I've been there!" Jenny exclaimed.

"I've only been to that city once. We lived on a ranch. To the southeast."

"A ranch," I said. "That sounds really nice."

He gave me another funny look, and I got the feeling I'd said something stupid, but I wasn't sure what.

"It probably was once," he mumbled. "I don't remember. My mom sent me and my brother here to live with my aunt. It's safer."

Just then the screen door clacked open and Miguel and Javier stumbled out, laden with provisions.

"Leave Tito alone for a minute, and he moves in on the ladies." Javier set the tray of foil-wrapped parcels on the other table. "Slide over, hey? Let's put these tables together."

Jenny and I exchanged a glance. Evidently these boys would be dining with us. She didn't object, and neither did I, so we shifted our chairs over to make space.

It was fun hanging around flirtatious boys, even if they were all circling around her.

Javier slid his chair next to Jenny, and Tito claimed the spot at the end of the table, so Miguel pulled a chair over by me.

Miguel filled three plastic cups with horchata, then produced two more cups. He looked to us expectantly, "Would you like some?"

I nodded.

"No, thanks," Jenny replied. "I don't care for cinnamon."

Javier clutched his heart as though mortally wounded. "You don't like cinnamon? I don't care now how pretty you are. I can't marry you."

Jenny didn't skip a beat. "Oh, good. That saves us the heartache of failed courtship."

"Saves nothing," he grumbled. "I will never even share a cup of Mexican hot chocolate with my true love. My sorrow is too great. I can never be happy again."

"Dodged a bullet there, Jenny," I said.

"You too?" he asked. "Even the quiet one insults me, as she sips the horchata my own mother has provided."

"You can't buy my affections with rice milk."

The three boys tore into the foil packets, which turned out to be leftover breakfast burritos.

"What about oatmeal? Can we buy your affection with oatmeal?" Miguel asked.

"How on earth did you know? Oatmeal is the currency for my esteem." I feigned shock and awe.

"Then you have to be nicer to me," Javier said. "Mami makes horchata with oatmeal. It's not traditional, but it's delicious."

"*Agua de avena,*" Tito said.

Jenny and I looked to him to elaborate, but he didn't.

We chatted for the next few minutes about the usual things. School—they went to Speer. Music—Miguel liked modern rock alternative, and Javier liked hip hop. Tito nodded and ate quietly unless forced to participate. I watched Jenny watch him.

I asked about Speer's volleyball team. The guys didn't know much about it beyond that the school had one, but Miguel came to life when I asked about Advanced Place-ment classes. He'd already passed AP English and Bio, and he'd be taking Calculus this year.

"See? You're going to be fine," Jenny said after she pulled up a page detailing Speer's twelve AP programs and ten concurrent-enrollment courses. "And the volleyball coach would be crazy if you didn't go straight to varsity."

I hated being the middle of this conversation, so I asked the guys about their extracurriculars, which pitted Javier and Miguel in an argument over cross country's merits versus those of team sports like soccer and lacrosse.

"I hate to break up this party," I announced after we'd eaten. I pinned a twenty-dollar bill under the Cholula bottle. "We've got another room to paint before this day is over."

Miguel looked from his friends to us. "Want help?"

"No, grasshopper," Javier said to Miguel, then directed to Jenny, "What he means is, 'Will you go on a date with me, if my friends and I demonstrate our gallantry by assisting you?' "

I froze. I was pretty sure dad wouldn't like the idea of me inviting three boys I'd just met into our home. But, with them helping, we could probably paint the whole second floor. Dad might be back at the house already anyway. And Jenny at least *kind of* knew Tito.

And they were so cute. Not that I was factoring that in or anything.

"It's Kassandra's house. And she can date you if she wants," Jenny replied.

Javier pulled another imaginary dagger from his heart. "She is so cruel, yet I am powerless under her spell."

Tito shook his head just a tiny bit, but Jenny noticed and rewarded him with a bright smile. Tito blushed and played with his straw.

Javier didn't notice any of it.

Miguel turned to me without changing his expression, awaiting my response.

"If you want." I shrugged. "Just, you know, promise to be careful. It's an old house, and I don't want to screw anything up."

"Woman," Javier said, "do you honestly think we can't paint? We can paint, drywall, and landscape. We're Mexicans."

I choked on the last sip of horchata in my cup, and tears sprang into my eyes.

"I don't know how to drywall," Tito whispered.

Miguel threw his straw wrapper at Javier, then said to me, "I'm happy to help. I was supposed to work today, but they cut me early. I just have to go home and change." He asked Tito, "You in?"

"Yeah," Tito said into his straw, not looking up.

"What's the address?" Miguel asked me, standing to let me pass.

I gave it to him, and his smile disappeared.

"At the corner of 38th and Grove?" he clarified.

I replied, "Yep, you can't miss it. Big yellow house. Broken porch."

He glanced to Javier, whose mouth had fallen open. "Yeah, I know the one."

Miguel set his jaw and took a step back, away from me. "Yeah." He drew the word out to be about three syllables. "You know, I don't think I'm going to make it."

Jenny and I exchanged confused glances.

She spoke up first. "Afraid it's haunted?"

Javier looked back to Miguel, as though waiting to take his cue.

"Yeah," Miguel deadpanned. All traces of his former cheerfulness had evaporated. He pushed his chair in and backed through the side gate. "Hey, listen, I just realized there's someplace I need to be. Good luck on your projects." He collected his skateboard, and took off down the sidewalk.

Javier and Tito shrugged apologetically and carried the dishes inside.

"Was it something I said?" I asked.

TEN

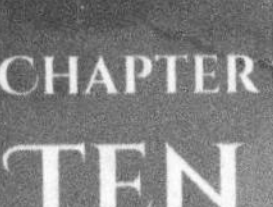

J enny and I tried to make sense of Miguel's attitude change as we walked back to the house. He hadn't seemed afraid of the house. He'd seemed angry.

We cranked the music again and started on the second coat of paint, but a knock on the door interrupted us.

Javier stood on the front step, his hands in his pockets.

"Hey," I said. "I didn't think you were coming."

Jenny rolled her eyes and marched back up the stairs.

He shrugged. "I don't want to miss my chance to impress the beautiful Jenny with my painting skills."

"I'm glad to see you then." I stepped aside to let him enter. "Can I get you a soda? We're out of Mountain Dew, but there's Sprite."

"Yeah, I like Sprite."

I grabbed him one, and there was another knock at the front door. This time it was Tito.

"Hey, come in. Is Miguel coming too?" I looked past him, but the street was empty.

"I do not think so," Tito said. "Hey, Javier. Not surprised you're here."

Javier grabbed a second soda can from the fridge and tossed it to Tito, who caught it about six inches from his face.

Rivals much?

I showed them the way to our workspace.

"Look, I don't want to put you guys in a weird spot with your friend," I said, "but you had to know I'd ask. What's up with Miguel?"

Tito looked to Javier, and it was clear he was deferring to him for the answer.

Javier dipped his roller into the tray and ran it back and forth a few times to get rid of the excess paint before he answered. He didn't meet our eyes as he spoke. "This is his family's home. He's never lived here or anything, but his great grandfather or something built it."

"Why did they move?" I asked.

He dropped his roller to his side for a moment and looked me in the eye. "I don't know. His *bisabuela* sold it."

"Where's he live now?" I asked.

He resumed his work. "Not that far from here. It's a housing project."

"Oh."

Jenny paused her trim painting. "So he's mad? That doesn't even make sense. It was supposed to be torn down before Kaz's dad bought it."

"That's a little insensitive, don't you think, Jen?" I said.

Javier shook his head. "The woman I love—she has a cold heart, and bewitching eyes. I'm doomed."

She flicked a wad of masking tape at him.

She caught Tito's eye when Javier reloaded his roller,

and Tito winked, sharing a secret smile. When she turned away it was Jenny who was blushing.

It must have given Tito confidence, because he broke the silence. "'Uela should never have sold the house. It was their protection and their birthright. Children pay for the mistakes of their ancestors."

We continued working for the next several minutes without further comment.

Javier finished the last wall and deposited his roller in the tray. He squatted next to the paint supplies like a cowpoke would squat by the fire to tell a story. He popped open and stirred the next can of paint. "When rich people move into poor neighborhoods, they fix things up and everything gets nicer. Then other people want to move there too, so rents go up, and it gets more expensive for the people who lived there in the first place. It's hard not to be resentful when things you want keep moving out of reach. Are we doing the hall next?"

I blinked, then stammered, "Let's do the guest room first—it already has one coat. Tito's almost done with the ceiling." I went in and laid out the tarp and Javier moved the supplies. Jenny was almost to her starting point at the doorway, so she'd catch up soon.

"Miguel resents me?" I asked while I swapped out the roller heads for clean ones.

He poured paint into one of the clean trays. "Look, I know about this house because Miguel is obsessed with it. Do you know how long he'd have to work his hardware store job to be able to afford what you're doing here? You get to live his dream, and you don't even know what you've got."

Tito rolled the final coat of white onto the ceiling.

I cut in around the doorway with a heavy swath of dove gray. "I do now."

"Right," he said.

"Gentrification." Jenny appeared in the doorway with her cup and brush. "My uncle is a developer, so he talks about it a lot."

"Huh?" Javier asked.

"That's what it's called when rich people buy up poorer neighborhoods. Sometimes they call it revitalization, but, yeah. It raises rents and pushes former residents out of a community."

"But we're not rich," I said.

"Yeah," Javier said. "Rich people usually say that."

ELEVEN

The next morning the house was crawling with workers. Plumbers replaced bits of pipe here and there. Roofers tore off layer after layer of patched roof, replaced the rotten plywood beneath, layered on new tarpaper and asphalt shingles. A structural engineer combed through the house and measured, snapped pictures, and made notations in his tablet.

"You've done good work in here, kid." Dad examined the new paint in the upstairs rooms. He peered into my closet, also freshly painted and bare, the wire and tension rod already in the dumpster. "What are you working on next?"

"I think I'm ready to build out the closet."

"Okay. Why don't you get a jump on that now? I'm going to need the chop saw in a bit, but you can go first."

"Deal," I said, snapping the clip on my new toolbelt. It was just a buckskin pouch on a wide nylon strap, but it still made me look badass.

I'd already written down my measurements, so I trotted out to the backyard to make the cuts. I'd lugged the lumber back through the house when there was a knock at the door, so I deposited the wood in the corner of the entryway, giving myself a splinter in my rush.

It was Miguel.

He was dressed in work clothes, dried paint splatters on his T-shirt, and an apologetic expression on his face.

"Hey. Come on in." I pulled the door wider.

He stood in the center of the foyer and took a deep breath.

We both spoke at the same time.

He said, "Kassandra, I'm sorry about the way I acted—"

I started with, "Javier told me about—"

We both halted, then sputtered out apologies.

I waited for him to continue.

"I got weird on you yesterday," he said. "It's not your fault."

"No, I totally get it. Javier explained what was going on."

"Yeah, of course he did. He's a traitor. It's not you. I'm not mad at you."

"You're at least sort of mad at me." I stuffed my hands in my pockets and leaned back on my heels. "And that's okay. My dad bought your house, and that's not cool. Maybe better than developers scraping it into the landfill. Still someone's messing with what your family made. I'd resent me if I were you." I plopped down onto the foyer bench and folded my hands in my lap. "No wonder you didn't want to hang out and discuss paint colors with me."

He sat down next to me and ran both of his hands through his hair—a gesture that was totally sexy from him —and exhaled. "Actually, I do want to hang around you and discuss paint colors. Or help. Or whatever."

I blinked twice. *Did he say he wants to hang around me?*

"I'm not going to pretend I don't have every intention of buying this house back from you someday. My great-great-great grandfather," he ticked off the three *greats* on his fingers, "built it with his own hands." He traced his finger along a carved leaf detail in the mahogany, then dropped his hand and gazed around him. "I'd never been in here until now."

"Oh, Miguel, I'm sorry."

"Listen, Kassandra, I want to help you work on it some. Get to know it, you know?"

"You don't have to offer labor just to see the house." I shrugged and turned my work boot onto its side, which kind of hurt my ankle a little, but it was something I couldn't not do sometimes. "You could just come and hang out."

"True. But I like doing this kind of thing." He knocked his brown knee against my golden one, and goosebumps immediately sprouted on my arms. "And there is a pretty girl who's been hanging around over here." His eyes smiled even as he tried to keep his mouth in a neutral position.

Is he talking about Jenny? My face warmed. *Or me?*

"And I had no idea how hot she could look with a toolbelt."

Me. He was talking about me. "Omigosh! I have something of yours." I jumped up, ran to the living room, and retrieved the two old photos from the sideboard.

I handed them to Miguel and seated myself next to him again to watch while he examined them.

"What are these?" He turned the yellowed squares over in his hands.

"I don't know. Jenny and I found them under the drawer in the sideboard the yesterday. I was going to research them at Central Library, but they're probably rightfully yours."

"That's really cool," he said. "I wonder who it is."

"Your relative for sure." I took the portrait photo and held it beside his face. "You two have the same eyes and nose. His jawline is a little more squared." I gestured to my own chin. "And your mouth is different. Your lips are fuller—"

The corner of his mouth twitched, and I realized I've stared at his lips a moment too long. I looked away and set the photo down before my sweaty hands could mar the surface.

When I glanced back, *he* was looking at *my* mouth—and very intently.

His chestnut eyes met my gaze, and he lifted his chin. He inclined his head slightly. The space between us shrunk. "So, uh." His voice cracked, and he cleared his throat. "I'll ask my grandmother about the pictures."

"Y-yeah." Another centimeter closer. He was going to kiss me, and the wait for it was the most delicious moment of my life.

"Hey, Kazoo!" The spell was broken by Dad's booming voice. "Could you come have a look at these?" He appeared in the hallway from the kitchen. "Oh. Sorry. I didn't know you had a guest." He blinked and cocked his head. "Miguel? How have you been?"

Miguel jumped to his feet. "Mr. West! Sir. I didn't— Is this your house?"

"Wait." I glanced from one to the other. "You guys know each other?"

They shook hands and Dad clasped Miguel on the shoulder with his other hand. "Miguel was in my class a while back. What grade are you in now?"

"I'll be a senior in the fall, sir."

"I guess it was longer ago than I thought."

I stood and fiddled with the pliers on my toolbelt because I didn't know what to do with myself while they were having their moment. "Um, Dad, Miguel's great-grandfather built this house."

His eyebrows raised. "Is that so? Did he build many of the homes in this area?"

"I think it's three 'greats,' actually. But no, sir," Miguel replied. "He was in mining. This was the family home."

"I see," Dad said. "Small world."

"Miguel offered to help out with some of the projects."

Miguel waited for my dad's permission.

"Okay," Dad said and glanced between the two of us. When his gaze settled on me, he nodded slightly and I realized he knew he'd interrupted something. "Don't mind me. I'll just be building cabinet boxes. In the garage. Where I also happen to keep a chainsaw and a shovel. So, hey, you kids be good." He turned and disappeared without ever telling me why he needed me in the first place.

TWELVE

My face burned with embarrassment. *Did my dad really just say that?*

"Sorry about that. He—" What could I say?

"Your dad is awesome. He's one of my all-time favorite teachers." Miguel ran his hand again through that wavy black hair.

My fingers twitched, itching to follow the path his had taken. My mouth went dry.

He smirked, completely unfazed. "All right, Boss Lady. What are we working on?"

"Um, I was just about to build out my closet. You know —shelves and hanging rods and all that."

I collected the lumber from where I'd deposited it in the corner. Miguel immediately took it from me, leaving me feeling super awkward with nothing to do with my hands.

"Um, can I get you something to drink?"

"Nah, I'm fine. Where do we take these?" He balanced the load like a pro. But then he did work in a hardware store, so I guess he kind of was one.

For a moment I was totally distracted, picturing him in a toolbelt.

He looked to me expectantly.

"What? Oh, this way." I shook my head to clear the reverie and the twinge of guilt—like he'd know what I was thinking.

It's not like I was imagining him naked.

And then, because the power of suggestion was so strong, I had to concentrate on not doing exactly that. I was not entirely successful.

He let me lead the way, and I had the distinct impression he was watching the backs of my legs as I climbed the stairs. I added a little extra movement to my hips, hoping it looked graceful and feminine and also that my legs weren't as red as my face probably was.

"That was weird, right?" I said while Miguel held boards and I fastened them to the wall. "You and Dad knowing each other, I mean?" We were doing a basic build, and I could probably have done it in my sleep, but I was a little flustered. And for good reason. I was standing in a tiny space next to a very attractive boy. I couldn't *not* be aware of his proximity.

He smelled incredible—like cinnamon and soap—and I kept thinking about what would've happened if my dad hadn't walked in when he had.

Miguel was going to kiss me.

He positioned the one-by-four over the markings—his ropey forearm muscles flexed while he waited for me to secure it. "Yeah. It is always weird when you run into teachers outside of school. I didn't know I was hanging out with Mr. West's daughter."

I changed the bit to a Phillips head and drove the screws in flush.

"You're good at this, you know," he said.

He blinked his impossibly long-lashed eyelids, and I felt his gaze as certainly as if he'd touched me.

My face warmed. "Yeah, well, my dad's a shop teacher. I've been playing in sawdust since before I could walk."

"And you like it." His shoulder bumped me and he grinned as he wedged the next board into place.

Emboldened in my badass toolbelt, I braced my arm against his to drive in the last two screws. I hopped off the step stool and lifted my chin defiantly, inches from his. "Yeah. I kinda do."

I ducked out to retrieve two more boards and heard him exhale.

Twenty minutes later the closet was finished and the two of us collected the extra screws I may or may not have dropped due to nerves.

"That was quick," Miguel said. He wrapped the extension cord neatly and handed it to me.

Two rows of one-by-fours supported new cedar shelves, which had wooden dowels securely fastened beneath for the hangers.

"Yeah, good work." I nodded. "A custom closet at a fraction of the cost, thanks to a little elbow grease and some wood from the good people at Front Range Lumber."

His arm brushed mine, and the hairs on my neck stood up. We were still in the tiny closet together. My confidence evaporated.

I hastily backed into the broader space of my empty future bedroom. "Wanna do the one in the next room too?" I looked out the window, pretending to have some curiosity for the weather or something, a move which probably looked just as awkward as it felt. I tapped my palms on the window frame. "I'm thinking just one shelf and hanging bar. It's a guest room, so it doesn't need as much storage—"

Miguel moved into the space next to me. He rested his hand on the frame and leaned his head into my line of vision. "Do I make you nervous?"

My eyebrows shot up, and a small, startled laugh escaped, but I didn't move away. "Yes."

He stayed there, inches from my face. The intensity of that chestnut gaze stilled my heart. "I like you, Kassandra West. Do you like me?"

My face burned and my skin tingled. *Is he going to kiss me?* "Um, yes?"

"Do you *like me* like me?" He grinned like an elementary school kid, his head tilted, smile widening. His teeth were perfect, except for one eyetooth on top, turned ever-so-slightly out of line. That one imperfectly aligned tooth made him absolutely perfect.

I swallowed the lump in my throat and repeated, "Yes?"

He nodded. "Okay then." He backed up and squared his shoulders in showy confidence. "Let's go fix that other closet."

"What was that?" I reached out to shove him playfully, but he caught my hand and held it for a second before plunking the tape measure into my palm.

My hand tingled where our skin had touched.

"What was what? I like you, and you like me. You're going to kiss me. But since I only just met you yesterday, I can see why you're holding back. I can be patient." He smiled his full, toothy smile again.

"You sure are confident, aren't you?"

He shrugged. "A pretty girl just told me she likes me."

One room over, when we stared into an empty closet, he

stood right next to me and our shoulders and arms touched. We were the same height.

"So just one shelf there?" he touched a fingertip to the back wall.

"Yeah. Or up here, so if we need to convert it to double hung someday, we won't have to raise the shelf."

"Okay." He nodded. "You know, this doesn't look like plaster." He stepped into the small space, which was only about two feet deep, and tapped on the side wall to the left.

"I didn't notice that." I tapped on it as well. "Feels like fiberboard."

I picked at a piece of painted-over metal sticking out of the wall, a heavy-gauge wire stub that had probably been a hook or something.

Miguel knocked in a horizontal pattern across the wall.

"Kassandra, there's no stud behind this."

I pulled on the piece of wire and it clicked.

He and I exchanged a look. I pushed the wire back in, and it clicked again.

"Let me see," he said, and I dropped my hand. He pulled it. *Click.* "It feels like a latch." He shouldered the wall and the paint around the edges cracked. He pushed one more time and the wall swung inward.

"*Jesucristo*," he said and stepped back so I could see.

It was a small platform and a dark, narrow stairway leading down.

"Holy hell."

THIRTEEN

"A hidden staircase? You have got to be kidding me," Miguel said.

"Your family had a little money to throw around, huh?" I gingerly pulled the string dangling from a bare bulb on the ceiling, but nothing happened. "This is a servants' stair."

"There's another stairway right there." Miguel pointed to the hallway, where the dark banister was visible just outside the bedroom door. "Why would anyone need two stairways, twenty feet apart?"

"This could have been a nursery or maids' room. It probably goes to the kitchen, so the nanny could get a bottle or something and not disturb the family by walking through the rest of the house."

I activated my phone's flashlight and aimed it into the void.

The passage was only about two feet wide, with steep wooden steps and bare plaster walls, crumbled away from the lath in places. There was no railing. After six steps, the treads angled to the right, so I couldn't see the bottom.

I placed my hand on the wall and tested the first step with my weight. It creaked, but felt sturdy.

Miguel grabbed my other wrist, and a tingle coursed through my arms from that contact to where my other hand met the plaster. I swore it felt like the wall vibrated when Miguel touched me.

"Are you going down there?" he asked.

I dropped my hand from the wall.

"Did you feel that?" I asked.

His dark eyes searched mine. He shook his head. "Feel what?"

I put my hand back on the wall and felt a tremor, like the wall inhaled a raspy breath. Unless it was my imagination.

"Touch this wall. Do you feel a vibration?"

He let go of my wrist, liberating my cell phone hand, and placed his palm next to mine on the wall.

We were quiet for a moment.

"Nope. What do you think it was? The motor for an attic fan or something reverberating through the walls?" he asked.

"No, it wasn't like that." But I didn't say what it was like. It was like the house shivered. Something in my shorts pocket was digging into my leg. I jammed my hand into the pocket and located the offending object—the fat little gear I'd found at Grandma's. I didn't know why I was still carrying it around.

I shone the light down the steps again.

"I'm coming with you," Miguel said.

"Okay, but if I get scared, you'd better get out of my way."

"You get scared? The way you started down here I thought you had nerves of steel."

I placed my weight carefully on each step, testing for softness or rot. "What? Like you're fine with finding a concealed staircase and not checking out where it goes?"

At the curve, the stairway made a U and stopped at a paneled door with an arched top. Nothing happened when I pressed on it. The hinges must have been on the other side, and it was probably bolted.

"Darn it," I said.

"No secret passage to the treasure room," Miguel said.

"I'm not going to be able to sneak down for midnight snacks if this door won't open."

We headed back up the steps, which I tried to do in a calm and measured fashion even though I kind of wanted to sprint back up into the bright light of the guest room. I just really didn't want Miguel to think I was a wimpy sort of girl.

We checked the kitchen below, and determined the stairs must have opened into the little alcove where the refrigerator stood.

Dad walked into the kitchen as we were pulling out the mid-1980s Kenmore. "What're you doing?" he asked, pulling a Coke can from the fridge while we were still moving it.

"Secret passage," I said.

"Cool." He opened his can and leaned against the counter, but his eyes went wide when I hooked the claw of my hammer through a metal loop on the wall and pulled, cracking an arch of plaster six-and-a-half feet tall and two feet wide. "Wait, you're serious?"

I yanked the door open. "Serious as a heart attack, Dad."

FOURTEEN

I stood in the gaslit intersection again, on the gravel street.

The stores were gone. Like, completely missing—nothing behind me but a gradually sloping hillside.

This time, only one house existed. One solitary old house in a copse of trees, surrounded by grassed lots, the natural topography of the entire ridge unobstructed except by the street and the gas lamps. My house. Light emanated from every window.

This was new.

I made for the front walk, but hesitated again below the porch step. The dream took over, and I became a spectator in my own body—observing through my own eyes, but no longer making the decisions.

My feet climbed the steps and I entered through the front door. To my left was the beautifully decorated parlour, but only my eyes moved to glance that way. My head and neck remained facing forward, and my legs carried me through the swinging hall door and into the old-time kitchen, furnished with two butcher's block tables, an enormous Hoosier cabinet, and a broad black stove.

I crossed directly to the alcove on the left wall and opened the door that hadn't been there this morning.

The latch clicked, and I ascended the steps, one hand lifting my voluminous skirts away from my boots, the other carrying a silver candleholder that I didn't remember picking up.

The door at the top was closed, but I flicked the latch and it sprang toward me.

At my feet, on the floor of the empty closet, was a small wooden box.

Almost as soon as I'd seen it, the periphery of my vision swirled, and the scene disappeared.

A crew of electricians would be rewiring the house all day, but I expected I wouldn't be in the way too much if I continued to paint.

Dad and I headed over to the house first thing.

I was dying to get behind the wheel of my old green truck some more, so I made excuses about wanting to explore a little later and we drove separately.

Dad parked out front, and I tucked in behind him.

"I want to get those cabinet doors stripped today," Dad said. "Maybe we can hit up the architectural salvage later."

"Great. What're we looking for?"

"Chrome hinges, so the new cabinets will match the old ones."

"It'd be cool to get glass pulls for them too," I said. "The ones on there are so eighties."

"What would you know about the eighties?"

"What would I know about 1901, but you trust my judgment on that, don't you?"

"Touché."

As we hauled our gear up the walk, I remembered last night's dream.

This time I entered the house under my own power, but I followed the same path, just to see it again. Glanced to the empty parlour. Then the swinging hall door, pinned open. The kitchen and its alcove.

I grabbed my paper-towel-wrapped brushes from the counter and climbed to the second floor by way of the entry stairs, which weren't nearly as dark and creepy as the ones behind the fridge.

I arranged my drop cloth and paints, but nervously eyed the closed door of the guest room's closet.

I used to have the exact same dream over and over, but the dreams had changed since Dad bought the house. What had been the point of last night's dream? What had been the point of any of them?

I set my brush on top of the still-closed paint can in the hallway, and crossed through the guest room, which sat in perpetual shadow with only one narrow window.

I'll have a quick look. In case there's something I didn't notice before. Like a small wooden box.

The floor was empty. The closet was exactly as we'd left it yesterday.

I shook my head and exhaled, only then realizing I'd been holding my breath.

I returned to my paint cans, popped the lid open on one and filled a plastic cup. I swept the second coat of Antique White over various sections of millwork in the two rooms, but I was thinking about the stairway.

Really, I had no reason to go in there. I couldn't shake

the feeling that it would have been a bad idea to go in right then. Like Dad wouldn't know where to find me if I got locked inside and suffocated to death. But that was idiotic. It wasn't airtight. Besides, I'd starve first, or die of dehydration.

I sighed and threw my brush onto the newspapers. There was nothing to be afraid of. I could go look just because it was there, and it was cool.

I wiped my hands on my shirt and marched across the room.

The stairway door popped open easily when I tugged on the broken piece of wire. I would have to replace that with a proper pull and a handle because getting the door to close all the way without one had been a bitch.

I touched my hand to the wall, expecting it to do something, but it was just a wall. The light from my phone illuminated the treads well enough for my descent. I made it to where the steps curved, but this time the air felt close. Stale.

It only took a dangling strand of cobweb to psych me out before I saw the bottom door.

I about-faced and scrambled back up the steps in such a hurry that my toes smacked into the top riser, knocking the plank out of place. It clattered onto the tread below.

Nice job, Kaz. You broke the house.

I stood at the top of the steps panting and shined my light around the stairwell. It was only the plank I'd kicked that was out of place. There was nothing to be afraid of.

I descended again and retrieved the piece, shining my phone's light at its edges to look for rot around the fasteners, but there were no nails in it. It must have just been wedged into place.

Shoddy workmanship for the servants' quarters.

The hairs on my neck prickled again.

Quit fooling around. Put it back and get out of here.

When I tried to push the plank back into place, something in the space under the tread caught my beam of light.

It was small, rectangular, and honey-brown in color. And I knew exactly what it was.

I extricated the small box, carried it into the bright, cheery comfort of my own bedroom, and settled myself cross-legged in a sunny spot on the floor.

The chest was the size of a cigar box, wide and kind of flat. A small, brass lock sat in the loop, but it was not clicked shut. It clinked as I sat it on the worn hardwood next to me.

Gingerly, I opened the lid. Inside was one small item. A delicate hairpin. A tiny, twisted wire French honeybee suspended from the tarnished curve. I picked it up, and as soon as my index finger connected with the dainty wings, my vision blurred.

I didn't realize I was falling until my shoulder and head smacked the floor.

FIFTEEN

My head pulsed with the vibration of a dissipating headache. Opening my eyes intensified it again.

The air was thick and acrid. It tasted like soap. Like gritty, dusty lye that choked my corset-restricted lungs.

Corsets again. The dreams.

But this wasn't like my other dreams at all. It was not nighttime, and it was not quiet. Birds hopped and chirped in the shrubbery, dogs barked, and I thought I heard chickens on the other side of the hedge.

I was on a white wrought-iron bench in a fenced-in courtyard with a stack of canvas-bound books on the seat next to me, one opened face down on my lap. *Latin.*

Green grass. Blue skies. Broad cottonwood leaves rustled overhead in the breeze. It would have been idyllic if not for the smog, which was the real difference between this and my other dreams. I didn't remember being able to smell or taste in them. Then again, I didn't think tasting air was something I could do in normal life either, where air wasn't visible. And green.

I coughed and, in covering my mouth, found light-weight, gray leather gloves on my hands—beautiful, with tiny silver flowers embroidered on their cuffs. I touched one to my cheek again, just to feel how soft it was.

This *was* a cool dream.

I sensed movement behind me and shifted around in my seat, making corset stays dig into my ribcage. The book slipped from my lap and landed with an indelicate thud on the grass.

Under an arbor on the opposite side of the lawn, a couple whispered on a bench identical to mine. The girl moved her hands as she spoke in gestures too large for her subdued tones, like she couldn't contain her energy.

She glanced my way and twitched her gloved fingers in a barely-perceptible wave. The corners of her mouth curved into an instantly likable saucy smile.

I was pretty sure I'd never met her before, except her eyes looked vaguely familiar. Her skin was light olive, her curly brown mane stacked under a tiny straw hat. She was dressed a little like Mary Poppins, in a high-necked blouse and long wool skirt. On her, it was charming and elegant.

I was wearing the same kind of rig. Gray wool skirt and God-knew-how-many petticoats. Long-sleeved blouse. In the middle of summer.

I pulled the gloves from my sweating hands, being extra careful not to aggravate the splinter I got yesterday. Funny that it was still there, on my thumb, in this dream.

I sneaked another peek over my shoulder. I could see only the back of the boy's head, but it was clear she had his undivided attention.

My cell phone vibrated, and I dug through the countless folds in my skirt until I pulled out a buzzing device that wasn't my phone at all. It was a little larger—twice as thick and heavy enough to be made of lead, although it looked like brass. In the center, a grid of articulating silver pinheads clicked into a pattern, spelling "1605 ALERT ACKNOWLEDGE OR POSTPONE?"

It vibrated again and kept vibrating.

There was only one button on the thing, so I pressed it. The gadget chirped and then stilled.

The pins dropped and rose again. "ACKNOWLEDGED."

Wait, what? What did I do? What did that mean?

I turned the thing over. The other side had a mother-of-pearl analogue watch face. It was like a metal pocket watch brick. I'd never seen anything like it in all my antique-store combing. I prodded the button and discovered it was a wheel that spun around, but also clicked when I pressed it. As I twirled it, the pins popped up and down. *Set alerts; Display; Deliver.*

I peeked over my shoulder again. The girl pulled a watch from the boy's vest pocket, gazed at its face, and returned it. She whispered something and nodded her head in my direction.

My scalp warmed in embarrassment. She was talking about me.

I rubbed my sweaty palms over the soft material of my skirt, which didn't dry them because it was a thousand degrees out, and I had at least four layers of heavy fabric to roast me. The gloves were pretty, but who wore gloves in this weather?

I tucked the metal brick back into my pocket and picked up the fallen book, then flipped its canvas cover open to the title page. *New Latin Grammar, Charles E. Bennett, MCMX.*

1910.

Well, that didn't prove much. It could be a century old.

But it did kind of look new—the pages crisp and pulpy smelling.

A shadow passed over me, and I gasped when I saw what had caused it. An enormous metallic blimp was passing overhead, barely high enough to clear the buildings. People stared out the windows of the gondola, and I was sure they could see me, which made me want to hide in the thicket of trees and brush.

An airship. A derigible or a Zeppelin—I didn't know the difference. I remembered reading about the *Hindenberg* and how they put helium instead of hydrogen in the *Goodyear Blimp* because hydrogen was flammable, but this colossal metal thing was most definitely not the *Goodyear Blimp*. It moved past the roofline and out of my sight.

The thick bitterness of the air caught wrong in my throat and I coughed into my elbow.

"Hazel, dear," the young woman said from behind me, "I'll be only a moment." They'd risen, and she was looking right at me while the boy collected their things.

I glanced around to see if there was anyone else she could have been talking to.

Who's Hazel? Wait—am I supposed to be Hazel?

"Kaz," I said. "I'm Kaz."

She frowned and touched the boy's sleeve. "I should get her home."

My gaze fell on the books beside me.

Are those mine? Am I supposed to do something with them?

I set the Latin book with the others.

The couple now stood right behind my bench. I still couldn't see the boy's face—he was entirely intent on the girl. I wished somebody would look at me that way, if even for just a minute. Like Miguel, for example. But then I thought of how he *had* looked at me yesterday, and my skin grew impossibly warmer.

The girl carried only a small cloth purse, but the boy had four books tucked under one arm. He removed two from the stack, handed them to her, and kissed her for several very long and awkward seconds, as they now stood only an arm's length from me.

I turned away, not sure what to do with myself. I put the gloves back on and rose, then stood stupidly waiting because I didn't know where to go.

Where the hell am I?

"Hazel," she said—and I was surprised she was keeping track of me, er, Hazel while that boy was hanging all over her. "Take your books with you."

I scanned the bench and ground for a bag to put them in. There was none.

What? I've got a brass alarm-clock-scheduler thingy, but a backpack is too advanced?

She broke away from the boy and looped her slim arm through the crook of my elbow. She was even taller than I was, but she looked like a teenager. Her rose-oil perfume was a welcome change to the bitterness of the air.

In a hushed tone she said, "I can't tell you how much I appreciate your help—"

"How much *we both* appreciate your help," the boy said, using the same stage whisper and finally turning to face me. Our gazes met, and my mouth fell open. He was the boy from the sideboard photograph. He was my age. And he was standing in front of me in real life.

"Help?" I repeated. *What am I supposed to be helping them with? What am I doing here with the boy from those pictures?*

"Without you, Raúl and I would have no time together," she said.

"Raúl," I murmured, and then said, "Don't mention it."

"Of course, we won't say a thing outside of the three of us. Come now." She tugged my arm lightly and cocked a wry smile. "We look quite clever with so many texts."

I tried to play it cool and copied her cheerful, confident expression, but my eyes darted around, desperate for familiarity.

She and I followed a few paces behind as Picture Boy—Raúl—led us along a meandering path and through a low iron gate. We squeezed between a pair of spruces and stepped up onto a flagstone platform alongside a brick wall.

At once, I knew where I was. I halted in my tracks to gape at it.

This was my backyard. Dad's *partio*. The side of our garage, er, carriage house. And that was the back of my house. The red brick wasn't covered by mustard-colored siding, and the trees were just saplings, but it was the same house. I felt its presence like a living thing beside me.

"Whatever is the matter with you?" the girl asked. "You're behaving so strangely today."

I blinked at her.

She shook her head and pulled me along.

Raúl didn't take us to the house—just through another low gate into the dirt alley. There were double carriage doors where the garage doors were supposed to be.

Raúl arrested our progress by catching the girl's elbow. He whispered, "Meet me on Monday. At the library?"

"Of course."

"I love you, Laurel."

She—*Laurel?*—lifted her chin and smiled. "I know."

He didn't appear to be the least bit offended that she didn't return the sentiment, just waved and latched the gate behind us.

Laurel and I picked our way to the corner, lifting our skirts clear of the dust and debris.

The air was even thicker when we emerged onto Grove Street. I wanted to cover my mouth and nose with my hand, but Laurel had one of my arms twined with hers, while my other hand had to hold the books and corral my skirt away from actual piles of horse manure.

I glanced back at my house twice to try and remember which houses were supposed to be on this street. Most of them were familiar, but there was so much space in between. The bungalows and duplexes were missing. They hadn't been built yet.

A cow raised her head to watch us move past.

Imagine. A dairy cow in Denver.

The street we were on was quiet, but the noise from the horse-and-carriage traffic and the *ah-ooh-gah* of a Model-T horn sounded from 38th, behind us.

I caught Laurel studying my face as we headed south along the sandstone walk, away from the shopping district.

"Are you feeling all right, little sister? You look as though you may be having one of your episodes."

Little sister? I'm an only child. You are a weird dream. "Episodes?"

I shifted my books to my other arm for a moment and tucked a strand of hair behind my ear. "I'm sorry, I just feel a little out of sorts."

She stopped our progress and handed me her books so she could rearrange the offending strand back into its spot, framing my face. In my way again. "It will pass."

Laurel unlatched an iron gate in front of a massive three-story mansion. The colossal structure had a tower, ornamental brackets, decorative cresting and finials along the ridge of the roof. I knew it as the dilapidated law office down the block from our house, only it was not dilapidated at all yet. It was stately and—for all its beauty—intimidating.

She held me at the gate for a moment longer, like she needed to get something off her chest. "It must be terribly awkward for you to have to sit with us," she said in a low tone. "I am sorry. I can't think of any other way. I'll tell Daddy soon. I promise."

"No big deal," I said, still not knowing exactly how I was helping, though it was starting to sound like I was the wingman to an illicit affair.

"You use the most peculiar phrasings sometimes." She released her grip on my arm.

We moved up the walk to the house, and Laurel said in a low tone, "Do you want to see what Raúl gave me today? It was his grandmother's."

She pulled a silver pin from the curls under the brim of her hat and handed it to me. "This."

It was the honeybee pin. I hesitated to touch it—and for good reason—because when I did, my vision blurred, and the weight of her arm against mine disappeared.

I was sprawled on my side on the floor of the bedroom, a thrumming ache in my head, the box inches from my nose. The instant I saw it, I pushed myself up and scrambled backward to the wall, where I shivered, eyeing it warily.

I had a bee-shaped imprint on my thumb from squeezing the hairpin so tightly.

That hadn't been a dream. I hadn't been sleeping.

"Da-ad!" I scrambled to my feet and, half-falling down the stairs, called again, "Dad!"

Dad's sawhorses were set up in the shade of the cotton-wood, immediately beside the iron gate to the alley. The same one I walked out just minutes ago with some girl named Laurel and that boy, Raúl, from the photo.

I burst through the back doorway.

Dad cut the power to his heat gun immediately and dropped it and his scraper. "Jesus! What's wrong? Are you okay?" He came around the sawhorses and grasped my arms at the elbows, his gaze darting over me, presumably looking for injury.

I suddenly felt very stupid. What was I going to tell him? I found a box and a hairpin and, oh yeah, I thought I just time-traveled to the past, and it was really smoggy there?

"Um, I want you to see something."

"You flew out here like a bat out of hell so I could 'see something'?" He blinked twice. "Is it a body?"

"No. Sorry. I mean, sorry I scared you. I found some-thing. Could you c'mere?" I pulled his wrist.

"All right. What've you got? More secret passages?"

I pranced like an excited Jack Russell, but didn't start yammering until we were indoors. But by the time we reached the top stair, I'd told him all about knocking one of the risers loose in the hidden stairway, and that there was something very interesting inside.

He followed me into my room and spotted the box in the center of the floor. "Ah, lookie there." He dropped to one knee and picked it up. "Looks like cherry wood. Pretty brass fittings. Too bad about the cracked wood by the hinge."

"It's cracked? I didn't notice that." I scooted closer to see.

He unlatched the hasp and lifted the lid. "Yeah, it's in pretty nice shape. Nice joining."

"Yeah, but—" I looked over his shoulder.

There was nothing inside the box. The hairpin was gone, and the inside was totally clean.

"Omigod, I must've dropped it." I patted down my shirt and shorts, then scanned the floor and made Dad move out of the way in case he was standing on it.

He wasn't.

I sat back and shook my head.

Had I left it in the box? I looked at my thumb, but it was barely red where the bee had left its impression.

Dad was standing with his arms crossed, watching my frenzied search. "You want to tell me what's going on?"

"A bee—" I trailed off.

He furrowed his brow in clearly communicated disbelief. "Mmkay. So, we could repair that crack, and you could use this for jewelry or something. Nice find, kid." He gave me a very patronizing pat on the head as though I were a Labrador Retriever.

The doorbell rang.

"That'll be the electricians." He handed the box to me. "Try to stay out of their way, all right?"

I gave him a look. "Dad, really?"

"I did it again, didn't I?" He tugged my ponytail. "Sorry. Sometimes I get in teacher-mode and forget how capable you are."

He headed off to let the crew in. And I was alone with the box again.

I didn't put it back under the step, but I didn't keep it in my bedroom either. I didn't really want it in my space. Instead, I placed the box on the floor of the guest-room closet, approximately where it had been in my dream the night before. But I left the door open. To keep an eye on it.

I tried to be productive touching up paint, but kept

stopping to search again for the hairpin. How could I have lost something like that? I'd checked every inch of my bedroom. It wasn't there.

Is it possible that it had just—disappeared?

Before breaking for lunch, I glanced into the guest room again, intending to peek into the box one more time. The closet door had closed itself or one of the workmen had shut it, and I was too nervous to open it.

SIXTEEN

I was out in the backyard with a bucket under the spigot cleaning my brushes and trying to calm myself down when the doorbell chimed.

Dad was in the garage, so I trotted through the house and got to the front door just as the bell rang a second time.

Any anxieties from earlier melted away when I opened the door.

It was Miguel. His face broke into a wide smile when he saw me.

Butterflies leaped in my stomach—not an altogether pleasant sensation, but I'd have been glad to feel that way all the time. It didn't make sense.

"I wasn't sure if you'd be here, but I didn't get your number yesterday," he said.

"Yeah, sorry. I was out back. C'mon in." I stepped aside, and he caught my hand.

"Can I kidnap you? I want to show you some old stuff my grandma has. Some of it's from this house. You interested?"

His house? OMG. He was inviting me to his house? But of

course, he was standing in mine. Though it was not like I lived here. Yet.

"Yeah. Let me tell my dad."

"Tell him it's across from his school. We can get lunch, if you haven't eaten."

"Okay." I trotted out back to get permission.

"You're going to be with Miguel Montaño?" Dad asked.

Miguel stood on the back doorstep and nodded politely when Dad looked over at him.

Dad nodded back.

"Uh huh." I pulled on the hem of my shorts.

He nodded again, that time his consent. "Keep an eye on the clock. I'm leaving before rush hour. I've got that school fundraising thing tonight."

"Thanks, Dad." I stood on tiptoe, and he stooped a little so I could kiss his scruffy cheek.

I hurried across the yard and collected my paint brushes to wrap them before I went.

Miguel waved to my dad and called, "Good to see you, Mr. West," and followed me back inside.

Moments later as Miguel and I passed into the front hall, he seized my hand again and spun me like a dancer. After one turn, he caught me and pressed his lips to mine, completely taking me by surprise.

By super-awesome, amazing, dizzying, all-the-glitter-of-the-sun-moon-and-stars surprise.

His lips were smooth, but firm, and I tasted cinnamon. His arms around me felt like comfort and I relaxed into him. I kissed him back, and had to remind myself to breathe so I didn't embarrass myself by passing out in his arms.

OMG, I hope my breath isn't gross.

He pulled back, still hanging on to my fingertips, and he studied my face like he wasn't sure how I'd react.

"I thought you were waiting for me to kiss you." I grinned.

"Yeah, well, I got impatient. It has been almost forty-eight hours since I met you. Tick tock." He took a deep breath and asked, "Are you offended?"

I answered with another kiss. My heart raced, and I was certain he could feel it. Standing there in the entryway, leaning into his sturdy frame, was dizzying.

He wrapped an arm around my waist, and the fingers of his other hand laced into my hair.

I could do this all day—though eventually the not-breathing might have gotten to me.

"C'mere. I have something to show you." I guided him upstairs to the guest room, where the fresh-paint smell still hung heavily in the air. His eyes widened, and he went straight to the little wooden box on the closet floor.

"What's this?"

"It was under the landing step in the servants' stairs." I almost told him about the hairpin and the vision, but I hadn't worked out a non-crazy-sounding version, so I abbreviated. "I had a dream about it." Which was true.

I handed the box to him.

A little pop of static electricity arced between his fingertips and the handle as he took it.

"Ow. What is it, a jewelry box?"

"I don't know. It may have been a tie box. It's pretty masculine."

We dropped to the floor and he set it in front of him.

"Careful, the wood is cracked by the hinge." I pointed to the damage.

The box was still empty.

I'd already searched my bedroom thoroughly, and I'd

nearly made peace with the unbelievable—the pin gave me a vision, and then it disappeared.

"Very cool," he said, closing the lid. "Tell me about your dream."

"Maybe later."

"Was I in it?"

"No, it wasn't that kind of dream." I blushed when I realized how that sounded, and he totally called me on it.

He affected a scandalized stage whisper and leaned toward me. "What kinds of dreams do you have about me?"

"I haven't had any dreams about you, so you can bring your ego back down a few notches—hey, weren't we going someplace?"

"Ouch. Subject change."

We climbed to our feet. And when he put the box back on the newly-built shelf in the closet, I couldn't *not* stare at the ripple of his back muscles under his T-shirt.

Had he dreamed about me?

"It looks really good up here." He indicated the freshly painted walls, woodwork, and scrubbed floors. "You've been working hard."

"It wouldn't be this far along without your help. And Tito and Javier's."

He jammed his hands into his shorts pockets. "I know I was jealous at first. About you living here. But I am actually glad it's you. You care about the place. Maybe almost as much as I do."

"Yeah, well, you sure got over that jealousy in a hurry." I pushed him with my shoulder and led the way downstairs.

"I had to," he said when we reached the entry. He took my hand. "I couldn't stop thinking about wanting to kiss you. Disliking you was getting in the way."

"Yeah, I'm pretty irresistible like that." I tossed my loose ponytail over my shoulder. I wasn't even sure how to move like a normal person while my hand was in his. Or think like a normal person, for that matter. "So, hey, lunch? My stomach is growling."

"Yep. Guzmán's?"

"Sounds good to me. I still haven't had the tamales."

"Then you haven't lived."

Midday summer heat was in full effect, but hundred-year-old trees kept the sidewalk shaded.

We walked right past my little truck.

"Do you—" I began, starting toward it.

"No. Let's walk. It's not that far. And I like walking with you."

"Okay."

We held hands and walked toward the city. My heart still hammered in my chest, but I concentrated on slowing my breathing and playing it cool so Miguel wouldn't think I was a weirdo.

I asked him more about the neighborhood and his school. I hadn't decided yet if I'd be starting there in the fall, but now that I knew a few people, it didn't sound as bad.

Señora Guzmán was clearing a table on the patio when we arrived. Realization dawned in her expression as she sized up the situation—the two of us arriving together, unaccompanied. She fussed around us, placing us at a secluded corner table and chirping about *novios* and *amor joven.*

My Spanish couldn't keep up, but I sure wished it could. Whatever she was saying made Miguel blush.

We ordered Cokes and tamales, then practically dove into the chips and salsa when they arrived. No ladylike pecking at a salad for this girl.

I asked, "Have you lived here your whole life?"

"Yep. Fifth-generation Denverite, sixth-generation Colorado native, on my dad's side. My mom was born in Mexico. You?"

"I was born in Littleton. This will be the first time I've moved ever. I was born, like, six blocks from where I live. My parents met in college in California."

Miguel feigned pulling a dagger from his heart, the same move I saw Javier use a few days ago. "Rich girl buys my house, steals my heart, and then confesses she's a Californian. Love and hate dance together along a thin, thin line."

I play punched his arm. "I'm not! I just told you I'm a Coloradan, and Dad's family is from here a few generations back. He was born in San Francisco, though. Yesterday you were acting like he was the coolest teacher you'd ever had, so cut the crap." I popped another chip in my mouth, then added, "And we're not rich."

"Your dad makes more in his one job than my mom makes in all of her jobs combined. You can afford my house, and I can't. You are rich."

I nearly protested that we could only afford the house because it was priced below its value, but stopped myself. That wouldn't help.

He was right. We were rich. We owned two houses at the moment, and when I went to college, my dad would probably pay for it. We weren't vacation-home-in-the-Hamptons rich, but he had a point.

We munched in silence for a minute.

"I was joking, you know. I'm trying not to be obtuse about this. I am glad it's not going to be torn down. When my grandmother heard, she was beside herself for days.

Swearing under her breath, cursing the developers and burning smudges."

"It must've worked," I said. "They went out of business."

"Did they? I didn't know. 'Uela will be amused to hear it. I just heard it was going to be developed into a modern cookie-cutter mansion, and then there you were."

"Way-la?" I repeated.

"'Uela. *Abuela*—grandma. She's my great-grandma though, but I've never heard anyone address someone as *bisabuela,* you know? It doesn't sound as affectionate."

Our tamales arrived, and Miguel took the opportunity to ask Sra. Guzmán what she called her great-grandmother.

"*Bisabuela,*" she replied and returned to the kitchen.

He shrugged. "Maybe it's just me. What would I know? I'm an American."

At that moment Javier burst through the front door. "*¡Amigos!* Why didn't you tell me you were here?" He pulled a chair up to our table. "And where is your beautiful friend?"

"At work, I think."

He helped himself to a chip. "Right. The salon. And Tito is right next door, probably moving in on my girl."

I didn't tell him Tito had already moved in on his girl. I knew for a fact that Tito had spent most of last evening texting with Jenny, so, yeah, they were probably a thing.

Sra. Guzmán appeared in the doorway, dishtowel in hand. "*¡Javier! Deja a mis clientes. ¿No ves? Es una cita romántica. Déjalos.*"

Miguel said, "It's fine, Sra. Guzmán. I can't stop by without saying hey to my friend."

But Javier was already putting his chair back.

"Maybe so," she said, "but he has *una montaña de trabajo.*"

Ten minutes later Miguel ducked inside for our bill and came out empty-handed. "She won't let us pay."

"No?" I said. "But we ate, like, twenty dollars worth of food."

"Naw, it wasn't that much. Not here. But she won't let me argue with her."

"Can I leave a tip at least?"

"If you leave it on the table where she won't see it until we're gone."

I pulled out a twenty.

Miguel stopped my hand. "That will offend her."

"It's all I have. Do you think she'd make change?"

"She doesn't have to." He pulled a five from an indestructible paper wallet printed like a Sriracha label. "I win. Don't argue."

I couldn't pass it up. "Sriracha, huh? That's hawt."

He grinned.

"Too cheesy?"

"Definitely. But lovable. Come on—I'm on a mission to show you amazing things."

On our walk to his house, he held my hand. We paused by a huge tree and kissed some more, and when we continued our stroll, I told him about my recurring dream.

"So, you had dreams about that house before you ever even saw it?" There wasn't a trace of disbelief to his tone. He sounded interested.

"Yeah. For like a month. And I didn't even know it was the same house at first because it looks so different."

He was quiet for a moment, then he squeezed my hand. "When we get to my house you should tell 'Uela. She's very interested in dreams."

"Okay," I said. I didn't tell him about Laurel and Raúl and my crazy experience this morning. There was no way to make that sound sane.

He directed me to turn left. A moment later, we cut along a diagonal sidewalk into a community of newly built apartments across the street from the middle school where my dad taught.

This is a housing project?

When Dad talked about it, I pictured neglected tenements with grubby children playing barefoot in an unkempt yard. This cluster of tidy apartments, flanked by small yards of clotheslines, brightly colored play structures, and swathes of lush green grass was not.

"This is pretty," I said.

Miguel led me through the door with an assortment of large terra-cotta pots on both sides of the stoop.

"'Uela, it's me." He dropped his hold on my hand.

A small figure shuffled from one of the doorways, and the hairs on my arms stood up before I even registered recognition.

"*Lo sé, Mijo,*" the bent old woman rasped.

It was the old woman I'd met on my street. The woman who prophesied at me in Spanish. That was Miguel's great-grandma.

In her hand she carried a small sweet-smelling bouquet of herbs, which she deposited on the hall table.

"'Uela, this is my friend Kassandra. Kassandra, this is my great-grandma, Doña Marta Moya."

She hobbled over and peered at me, then looked point-edly at our hands. Though we were no longer holding hands, I had the distinct impression she knew we had been. Her eyes crinkled in a motherly expression.

"Hello, little one. *La avellanita, ¿no?*"

So she *did* speak English—and like a Colorado-born local, which Miguel had said she was. She just dosed it up pretty heavily with Spanglish.

She reached up—I was probably almost a foot taller than she was—and touched my face. She stared into my eyes, and it was super-awkward. I didn't know where to look.

My gaze finally settled onto hers. Her eyes were so dark I couldn't make out the edges of her pupils.

She pulled an egg from the pocket of her skirt and, grasping my arm, tugged on it until I stooped down. She patted my head with one hand, then passed the egg over my head, touching it briefly to my scalp, then moved it in a circular pattern over my shoulders and arms, all the while muttering in Spanish. When she finally stopped, she stared at the egg, then spoke to me in English.

"Little one, you have a tangled soul." She gestured toward Miguel. "Like his."

We exchanged a glance and he raised one shoulder slightly, apologetically.

Miguel said, "Kaz lives in *la casa de la familia*. And she's had prophetic dreams you might have fun interpreting."

'Uela didn't look up from the egg. "I know about the house. I know about the dreams. I told her she has the eyes."

She pulled my wrist again, moving me away from the doorway, and brushed past me. She dipped her fingers into a water glass on the side table, flicked the droplets onto the egg, then took the glass and the egg with her out the front door.

"Come look at these," Miguel said.

He took me to an ornate bookshelf in the corner of the living room, and I recognized the carved-leaf pattern from the built-ins in our house.

I knew why Miguel brought me to see this. The five shelves were stacked with antiques—a collection of small, leather-bound books; family albums; framed sepia-tinted photos; squat bubble-glass apothecary jars; and an ornate, hammered-copper box. I'd only known Miguel for a few days and already he knew what I geeked out over.

There, tucked under the corner of a bud vase, were the photos from the sideboard, pictures of the guy I'd talked to in person just this morning. Miguel pointed to the portrait. "This is—"

"Raúl," I whispered.

"Yeah." He gave me a funny look. "You looked him up? My great-great-great uncle. 'Uela's uncle. Raúl Cienfuegos. His father built the house."

I snapped a photo with my phone, and took one of the class shot, as well.

Raúl and Laurel. It hadn't been a dream. Those were real people. And they'd lived, like, a hundred years ago. *Wait. What could I possibly have been doing in their world a hundred years ago?*

I shook my head and blinked several times, but the confusion remained just as unsettling.

"What are these?" I pointed to the books.

"My great-great-great-grandmother's journals. They're like recipe books for healers." He took the top one from the stack, untied the leather strap, and handed it to me—

smiled when I recoiled. "It's okay, you can touch them. I trust you to be careful."

The cover was warm to the touch. I opened the tiny volume to its center. They were handwritten in old-fashioned penmanship, mostly in Spanish. *Empacho. Susto. Esterilidad. Bilis.* Some of the instructions went on for two or three pages. Each leaf in the book was decorated with a printed pink rose.

There were five more of them standing between book-ends on the shelf. "Are they all like this?"

"Yeah. All hand-written. All filled to the last page."

"Can you read them?"

"Yeah, mostly. Except for the ones that aren't in Span-ish. But it's hard to decipher the handwriting."

The front door opened, and his grandmother shuffled back in. This time her expression was troubled. "You must go."

"'Uela, we just got here."

"*Necesito pensar. Y ella tiene que irse.*" She took my arm and guided me out the doorway, but had her shawl wrapped over her hands like she didn't want her skin to make contact with mine.

"'Uela—"

"*Tú también. ¡Vayan afuera!*" She swatted him with her shawl.

He shook his head, turned his back to her and stalked out. The door slammed as soon as he cleared the doorway.

For a moment we stood there on the step, confused.

"So," I said slowly. "I should go."

He grabbed my hand and held me in place next to him. "Kaz, I'm very sorry. She does this sometimes. We humor her, but usually she isn't rude."

"Really, it's okay. I'm not offended."

He pulled me into a hug, then left an arm around me as we walked toward the street.

"The other day when I met her, I thought she didn't speak English. But she was born in Denver, right?"

"Yeah," he said. "Spanish is the language of her ancestors. I think she uses it when she wants them to hear. But she and my mom have always prioritized Spanish at home so I'd have a chance to learn."

The door opened again, 'Uela in the doorway. She hurried down the step and, taking my hand, pushed an ornament into it.

"*Para tú protección*." She closed my fingers and patted my hand, then crossed herself and retreated into the house, firmly closing the door behind her.

I raised an eyebrow at Miguel who took my hand to see what was inside it.

"Oh, yeah. I have one of those. *Mal de ojo*." He pulled one from his pocket. Like mine, his was a small bright blue bead with a black dot inside a white dot—a tiny bright eyeball—and also a red-brown clay disk the size of a quarter, etched with the squiggly ring-shape of a snake eating its own tail. Two brackets around the centered hole made it look like an eye. A thumb print was visible on the pressed wafers, and I wondered if his grandmother had made them herself. Both of our charms were tied with red ribbon, but a key dangled next to his.

"It's a keychain?"

"Not really." He returned his to his pocket and slipped mine over my hand onto my wrist, retying the knot tighter. "It's supposed to be against the skin, so they're usually around the neck or wrist."

"Why don't you wear yours?"

"I don't know." He sighed. "I get sick of her waving

smudges at me and tucking charms in my pockets, so I follow a little less carefully. You know? And because the strand broke."

"You're such a rebel."

He bumped my shoulder with his. "Does that impress you?"

Be cool, Kaz. Do not act like a fangirl. "Terribly. But what's it for?" *There. That devil-may-care absence-of-wit was super attractive.*

"Supposed to cleanse the blood, but I'm pretty sure that my liver and kidneys do that. Call it decoration." He raked both hands through his hair.

We walked back to my house and sat in the shade of my front porch together. He held my hand, a strange expression on his face. He kept looking at me and then looking away.

"What?" I asked.

"I want to kiss you."

"Oh, okay. You can kiss me." I laughed, and my pulse quickened.

We were both smiling when he leaned in. I met him maybe less than halfway. The kiss felt funny at first, our mouths curved up in the corners, but I relaxed into it.

He smelled like a boy, but in a good way. Like peppery soap.

I could do this all day.

When he pulled away, we were both still smiling.

"Can I call you?" he asked.

"Yeah. If we're gonna swap spit, I guess it's okay to swap numbers." I held out my hand.

He gave me his phone, and I programmed in my number, then sent myself a text so I'd have his.

"I'll call you this evening, okay?"

"Okay."

He kissed me one more time, just a quick peck, then backed down the walk, both of us grinning like happy idiots.

I turned around, absolutely thrumming with nervous energy. I stretched my arms over my head, spun in a circle, and kicked a pile of leaf litter into the air.

Omigod, what is that?

Carved into the bottom of the porch support, was a snake eating its own tail, an eye at the center of the circle. Just like the charm on my bracelet.

There was no paint left on the gray wood, and it was split in several places, but none of the fractures intersected the carving. That remained smooth and whole.

It's for protection.

The house is protected too?

That was a comforting thought, until I wondered what we needed to be protected from.

SEVENTEEN

I wasn't going to be getting anything done, that was for sure. I had way too much to think about.

Nothing would help me with my Miguel questions, but about Raúl and Laurel I might be able to get some answers.

I brought it up after we'd hauled the antique stove up from the basement and placed it along the back wall of the kitchen.

"Dad, would it be okay if I bailed on the architectural salvage trip? I want to hit up the library and look up some stuff on the house."

He shrugged and pulled a new gas line from the most recent hardware-store bag. "No big deal to me. I'm going to head out soon. I want to look for those hinges, but I need to get cleaned up before the Boettcher dinner tonight. Are you having dinner at Jenny's?"

"Nah, I'll just grab something on my way home."

"All right." He pulled a twenty from his wallet and handed it to me. "Take this. You shouldn't have to use your own money to buy food yet."

"Dad, I don't need twenty. I'm going to hit up a drive through, not a lobster restaurant."

"Take it anyway." He kissed my forehead. "Love you, kid."

"Love you too, Dad."

I navigated my little truck through side streets toward the heart of the city to Central Library, but took a little detour south on Broadway. I had more than one type of research to do down here.

I had to park two blocks away, but I didn't care. The OPEN sign was in the window at Stan's Antiques, and he only worked when he felt like it.

Must have been my lucky day.

A bouquet of cowbells on the pushbar announced my arrival, and Stan looked up from whatever gadget he was working on at the side counter. The place was crammed full from floor to ceiling with brass instruments and glass vacuum tubes. Stan specialized in scientific tools. We shared a similar brand of nerdy.

"Kassandra! How the heck are ya?" His dark comb-over flopped in front of his wire-rimmed glasses, but he jerked his head and it flicked back into place.

"I'm good, Stan. You?"

"Fine. I'm fine." He blew debris off the top of the tarnished metal triangle he was manipulating. "Here for a look around? Got some more tools. Mostly plumbing-related in that batch. And I've got a box of welding goggles just in, too. They're on the floor by the back room."

"Don't tempt me," I said. "Actually, I'm looking for something, but I'm not sure what it's called. It's a little brass box about this big." I made the dimensions with my hands. "And it has a watch face on one side and some little pins that go up and down to spell out stuff on the other side."

He set down his work. "A CommuniClock?"

"I don't know. What's that?"

"What you described. I don't have one though, and it wouldn't work if I did. Dangerous little boogers, those were."

"How could that have been dangerous?"

"Radioactive. They didn't used to know that stuff'd kill you. Radiation burns. Nope, I've got enough hazardous materials in here, what with the lead and the mercury. I don't need that."

I chewed on my bottom lip and drummed my fingers on the wood trim of the display counter. "CommuniClock, huh?"

"Yep."

I wandered over to the crate by the back doorway. "Gawd. You know me well, Stan." There must have been a dozen pairs of goggles, some in mediocre shape, but most with the leathers rotted through. I fished out a pair that looked okay. "How much are you asking?"

"The cosplayers can have 'em for fifty bucks apiece. But for you—five. I got 'em for a song."

I slipped them onto my head and tightened the strap. "Can't turn down a deal like that, can I?"

"If you're going to wear those on your head like a fashion accessory, least let me wipe them down. No tellin' what's on them. Give 'em here."

I did, and while he doctored them, I extricated the twenty Dad gave me.

Stan sprayed and wiped the lenses, then ran an oiled cloth over the leathers. They looked gorgeous.

"Need anything else, little britches?" He made change from an ancient register, and I shook my head.

"Good to see you, Stan. Take care."

"Try not to be so scarce."

"I will if you will." I pointed to the store hours sign, on which he'd written *Do you feel lucky? Well, do ya, punk?*

Stan's snort was cut off by the cowbells' clang on my way out.

Seven minutes later the elevator doors opened to Denver Central Library's fifth floor, the Western History/Genealogy section. Two gray-bearded gentlemen occupied the information desk, both tapping away and peering through their spectacles at the computer screens. At my tentative approach one cheerfully asked, "What can I help you with?"

"I, um, I'm looking for information about my house's history?" It wasn't really a question, but my uncertainty made it sound like one.

He returned his attention to his screen and said, "One of yours, Dale," to the other man, who perked right up.

"Building history?" the edges of his mustache pulled upward with his smile, and he hurried around the counter. "Is this your first time researching with us?"

"Yeah. I mean, I've done research, obviously, just not here."

"We love newcomers." He motioned for me to follow him to a cabinet of giant books. Each volume was literally as tall as my arm was long. "These are the Sanborn Fire Insurance Atlases. Do you know what year your house was built?"

"1901."

"Ah. You've got two editions to check, one from 1930, and another from 1904." He handed me a colorful map in a plexiglass stand. "Find your neighborhood on there and tell me what number you need."

"Six?"

"Very good." He pulled out a hefty volume that was almost as wide as it was tall, and, after laying it with great care on the table, we found the page with my house on it. In 1904, it occupied a quarter of the block, only sharing the section east of the alley with three other houses.

"There was almost nothing else there," I said.

He peered at the map and thought for a moment. "Potter Highlands. You probably have a bunch of nineteen twenties bungalows around you now, hmm?"

"Yeah, and a fifties duplex next door."

"A fifties— Say, you know a bit about houses, do you?" He tapped the page with an index finger. "These earlier homes sometimes sat on a parcel that was ten or twenty lots' worth, but in time, most of the owners subdivided and sold off land for development. Urbanization laws made it illegal to keep a family dairy cow in city limits, and the Model T was less expensive to maintain than a horse and wagon. They didn't need the pasture space anymore."

I pulled out my phone and snapped a picture of the page.

"This is the property here?" he asked.

"Yes."

"Okay, well, that street used to be called Landry Court. Here, snap a copy of that address, and let's find out about the people who lived there, shall we?" He guided me past a shelf of fat maroon books. "If you want to know who lived there after 1926, you can search through these, but the

Householders' Directories don't go back any further than that."

"Oh, wait, I have the builder's last name."

He put his hands on his hips. "Why didn't you say so? What's the surname?"

"Cienfuegos. I don't have his first name, though." I suddenly felt just a little bit skeezy. It occurred to me that this was just another type of Google stalking. I was researching Miguel by way of his family history, and using the house as an excuse.

But it's the house's history I'm looking for, I convinced myself. *Miguel being involved was only coincidental.*

I jammed my hands into my back pockets.

Dale indicated the bank of computers. "Then we'll go straight for the census records. Fortunately, most of those are available online now, so let's start there. Ten years ago, you'd have been searching the microfiche slides yourself, and you'd probably have given up before finding what you wanted."

He told me to sit in front of a keyboard, but leaned past and after a few taps said, "There. 1910 U.S. Census."

I clicked where he told me to. A PDF of a spreadsheet hand-written in pointy penmanship opened. Next to the yellow-highlighted address it said *Cienfuegos, Horacio. Head. Mx. 36. M. 18. 1. 1. Colorado. Spain. Mexico. English. Business-Mining. E. Yes. Yes. No. O. F. H.*

I consulted the legend for the translation. Horacio was thirty-six. Married for eighteen years with one kid. He was born in Colorado. His mother was born in Mexico, and his father in Spain. He spoke English. He was a businessman in the mining industry and an employer. He could read and write, hadn't attended school in the previous calendar year, and he owned his house.

I read on. His thirty-three-year-old wife's name was Perla, and his seventeen-year-old son was Raúl.

"Now that you've got a name, you can search other public records. You don't need my help for this. Use the search engine. Plug in the names and see what you find." He patted me on the shoulder and wandered back to his swivel chair and computer screen.

I searched "Horacio Cienfuegos, Denver," and the page filled with articles.

Whoa. This guy was popular.

The first page was a Wikipedia article about the company Standard Solarum.

I skipped down to the part about Horacio. He'd owned the two largest solarum mines in Colorado, and he'd partnered with a Mr. Seathan Scott, whose expertise was in refining and distribution. Together they'd founded the company, which was only in business from 1901-1911.

Next article. This one was a scanned image of the actual newspaper page with the headline SOLARUM COLLAPSE! It explained the bankruptcy of Standard Solarum and repercussions of the mine and refinery closures on the state's economy. Demand for the mineral had ceased almost entirely after scientists released reports definitively linking several maladies and even deaths to contact with the mineral.

That explained how Miguel's family used to have a lot of money, and now they didn't.

I vaguely remembered learning about the solarum industry collapse in Colorado History, but that was fifth grade and it seemed like a million years ago. Mining history wasn't really my bag. Funny I hadn't heard about CommuniClocks and other solarum-powered gadgets until now though.

My phone buzzed. It was Grandma. "Hi, baby girl. Busy?"

"Um, no, not really." I printed the newspaper article and logged off. "Do you miss me already?"

"You know I do. Listen, I was more efficient than I thought I'd be, and I can knock a couple of bucks off my flight if I switch it to midweek. I'm coming in tomorrow, late afternoon."

"Gram, that's great!" I had to whisper my enthusiasm. The room was quiet and I didn't want to broadcast my conversation for everyone to hear.

"Did you save any work for me?"

"You have no idea." I laughed.

"What about you? How are you doing?"

I groaned. "I don't know. You're going to be here tomorrow—let's talk about it then."

"Okay. I won't keep you."

After we hung up, I thanked Dale for his help and settled up my printing costs. While riding the elevator down, I did a search on solarum with my phone. Predictably, Wikipedia was the first result.

Solarum was a radioactive primordial element. It was mined primarily in Brazil, but was discovered in western Colorado. It was used in nuclear reactors, but historically was used to power steam engines. It burned like coal, but gave off a steadier heat for twice as long.

I pocketed my phone and arrived at my truck just as the parking meter clicked to expire.

Perfect timing, except a nervous tingle stole over my flesh and made the blinking red light feel just a little like a warning.

EIGHTEEN

The moment I set foot in the front door, I sensed the shift in the house's energy.

Like it was drawing me in.

I took the steps two at a time. I knew, I just knew, there was something inside the box again.

And there was.

It was another piece of jewelry—a gold necklace with two diving birds, swallows, connecting a delicate chain to the center of the most amazing locket pendant. A very complex, whirring locket. The glass outer dome covered an array of slowly spinning, tiny gears with a glowing pink gem in the center.

I reached for it automatically, but stopped myself just in time, and grabbed my phone instead. After I snapped a couple of photos, I braced myself and picked up the necklace.

Just like last time, my peripheral vision blurred, but I wasn't aware of falling. Instead, I paid attention and felt like I was rocketing upward in a super-fast elevator. I braced myself for the roller-coaster drop on the other end, but it never came. The deceleration messed with my brain, and a wave of sleepiness swept over me. I couldn't fight it enough to keep my eyes open.

I was out, and then I wasn't. The world was still again, and I didn't know how much time I'd missed.

I was still dizzy, but my head cleared when I shook it. I was bolt upright next to Laurel on a settee in a paneled hallway, dust particles dancing in sunlight that angled into our laps through the stained-glass entry.

She was speaking in a whisper. "Father came outside yesterday just as Raúl was leaving. He hasn't said anything, so I'm not sure what he saw." She twisted a handkerchief in her lap, then shoved it into her sleeve as though it had been the linen square that was the offending source of her anxious thoughts. "Of course, if he doesn't say something and he *did* notice, that could indicate that he doesn't mind. Don't you think he would bring it up if he noticed?"

"Um—I guess I can't say. What—um—what did he almost see?" I ran my palm over my cinched torso. There was that nasty corset again. I couldn't slouch if I wanted to. I'd have stood up to relieve some of the bind if I didn't think Laurel would find me rude, getting up in mid-conversation to tear at my clothing.

"I've decided to tell them after the holiday. Raúl will be eighteen by then, so it won't matter what they think."

I wrinkled my nose and shook my head in disbelief. "Um, if you're still seventeen, I think it does matter what they think."

"Hazel, it's so unbecoming to say 'Um.' " She squeezed my chin. "Are you having another episode? Your pupils are dilated. Are you disoriented?"

Of course I was feeling disoriented. I didn't know where the hell I was, when the hell I was, and what the hell I was wearing. My torturous clothes were neither designed to stretch nor to wick away body heat and sweat.

I wasn't in the house at 38th and Grove—this one was far grander. The law office mansion we'd walked to, perhaps? The stairway in the center of the room opened directly toward the front door, with halls of doors on either side.

"I can't say I feel my best at the moment," I said.

Her eyebrows knit together in concern. "You should go lie down. You're probably overwrought."

A bell right next to me jingled, startling us.

I stared at it for a moment as it danced, then registered the cord threaded along the molding and through an eyelet above the transom.

Doorbell.

Laurel rose and offered me her hand, so I took it. "Stand here and—try not to speak with that odd affectation."

She stepped around me and opened the imposing front door. What was that, honey maple? The inlaid woodwork was amazing. Dad would love to see this.

"Mr. Cienfuegos," Laurel said. "Please come in."

The man who stepped into the hall and swept his gray top hat from his head wasn't Raúl. He was middle-aged, with creases next to his eyes and worry lines on his brow.

"Is Father expecting you?" she asked.

"I believe so." His voice was baritone, and it was raspy like someone had frayed its edges with a file.

"Hazel, darling, please entertain Mr. Cienfuegos in the parlor whilst I announce his arrival to Father."

When Mr. Cienfuegos turned to me—and away from her—she shook her head, her lips closed tightly, and pantomimed fastening her mouth shut with a key. With her eyes still wide in warning, she brushed past me and down the hallway.

Entertain him, but don't talk. Perhaps I'll tap dance then.

"Miss Hazel, dear. It is good to see you well." He gave a small bow.

What's wrong with Hazel, anyway? Besides having me in her body, that is.

"Thank you," I replied. Certainly I was allowed to say at least that, as it would be extra peculiar for me to have gone completely mute. There's a sitting room on the other side of the stairs, so I nodded toward it to indicate that was where we should go.

He did, and I followed him, passing the entry table on which rested a folded newspaper—*The Denver Post, 22nd of September, 1911.*

My breath caught, and I choked on the bitter air.

Mr. Cienfuegos looked up in alarm. "Miss Hazel?"

"I'm fine," I stammered. "Please, forgive me."

I was almost immediately rescued by Laurel's return, along with the arrival of the man who was presumably her father.

My father.

Hazel's father, at any rate. Seathan Scott.

"Horacio, good man. You are prompt indeed." Father clasped his entire forearm in a handshake. "Thank you, daughters. We'll withdraw to my study so as not to bore you with details of business. I'm sure you must have engagements of your own." He turned on his heel, and Mr. Horacio Cienfuegos bowed to us again, then followed.

Raúl's class photo had 1911 written right on it, and my library research corroborated that. There was no reason to react this way now, except for the part where it was effed up for me to be here.

Laurel grabbed my hand and pulled me to the stairs. She whispered, "Hurry. I want to listen. If Father knows about Raúl, he'd mention it to Mr. Cienfuegos."

At the top of the stairs we cut across a sitting area, down the hall on the right, to the room in the farthest corner of the house, Laurel leading, and me following obediently.

It was a corner room with two windows, furnished with a brass twin bed with a lacy coverlet, a wardrobe, a dresser with a mirror, and two wooden chairs.

Laurel closed the door behind me, then dug in the top drawer of the dresser. She retrieved a brass funnel the size of a party hat, shook a curly cord from it, and fastened the cord to the pointy part. "Give me your CommuniClock." She beckoned emphatically. "Hurry, I want to hear what they're saying."

I extricated the little brass pocket brick, which she snatched from my hand.

She connected the other end of the curly wire into a port I hadn't noticed on the device before, and it immediately produced a staticky squeal. When she set the funnel on the floor at her feet, the squeal quieted. It fluctuated in pitch as she spun the wheel. Then, like she's dialed in a radio station, voices replaced the static.

Her father's voice. "—*What it means for our families. I see our immutable alliance as mutually beneficial.*"

Laurel's and my eyes widen. She mouthed, "Raúl?"

I shrugged, too busy yanking at my corset, but not making it any better.

She motioned for me to turn around, then untucked my blouse from the back of my skirt. With practiced dexterity she tugged at the strings of my corset and its grip on my middle loosened.

I exhaled gratefully. I was probably bruised where the stays had dug into my ribs.

"Better?" she whispered.

I nodded.

"Lie down then. Your eyes still have an odd look about them. You don't want to be ill."

He continued. *"Solarum has made petroleum a much more lucrative and promising investment."*

Her face fell. It didn't sound like they were talking about Raúl. She turned her back to me so I could loosen her stays, which I did, but with considerably more difficulty. She finally reached back and tugged her strings loose before throwing herself across the bed, seemingly less interested in the conversation since they were not talking about her.

"Our father and Raúl's are partnered in solarum? This can't turn out well. Their company goes under in 1911."

"Not likely. Investors have been scrambling to get a piece of Standard Solarum. We've never been so secure. When Raúl and I have babies, they'll grow up with the very best."

"Now that we're treating solarum with petroleum, the doubled burn time outstrips any other fuel source. It doesn't make sense to burn anything else. That's all thanks to you. You're a genius, Horacio. I'm even going to speculate with some of my personal funds in addition to the company monies we've already allotted. We can both feel safe investing our interests in Standard Solarum."

I lay on the bed next to Laurel. She was fidgeting with the CommuniClock thingie, but she left it connected.

"I'm not so certain," Horacio said. *"I believe there's basis for the public's concern regarding the safety of solarum."*

Laurel's brows knit together as her father's laugh rumbled from the device. *"Basis? Nonsense. It's no more harmful a mineral than coal. Safer even! It's significantly cleaner. Those men cough because they smoke, and the blisters on their hands are from an honest day's labor swinging the pick-axe. They'll toughen up."*

"With all due respect, I've seen them myself, and the blisters aren't friction burns."

"Horacio, good man, your concern for your miners is admirable, but—" Something heavy made a thud. A chair on the hardwoods, maybe? *"Good God, are those what I think they are?"*

"I haven't swung an axe in ten years, and yet—"

Laurel's worried expression met mine.

"What makes you so certain?" Father asked.

Horacio ignored the question. *"I think we should fund the researchers."*

"Good man, do you hear yourself? What of your family? Your investments? If the reports are confirmed, we'll both go broke."

"But if it is the rock, we can't continue to endanger the men, nor our customers. Solarum is in every home in this state, and hundreds of thousands more across the country. What if our own children are affected? What if your daughter's episodes—"

"We'll get to the bottom of it. If it is the rock, of course we'll prioritize the safety of your employees and the public. First, we need to secure our assets."

"The newsmen on our case are going to make the connection when I report for treatment."

"Then divert some of your investments to seek private treatment. That will buy us time to get the business squared away."

"We need to move quickly. The boys at the mine aren't safe, and we don't know the effect it has on the average man. I don't feel right keeping this to ourselves."

"One week," Laurel's father said. Footsteps. *"Keep it*

suppressed for just one week while we reorganize, and then we'll set up a press conference. Hold it together, good man."

A door closed.

Laurel switched off the receiver. For that moment we sat in silence.

"How did you know?" She pushed the side panel of the CommuniClock, and it popped open. A thumbnail-sized pink rock rolled out onto the coverlet.

"I read it."

"I read those articles too, but I took them for competitors' envious propaganda."

"It's radioactive," I said, but she probably didn't know what that meant. "It causes cancer."

"But it's everywhere. Are none of us safe? Do you think it could be what's been making you sick?"

I raised my eyebrows. "Am I sick?"

"I mean your episodes. If solarum causes coughs and lesions—"

"Those are men who work with it. Miners."

"And aside from them, whom can you think of who has more contact with solarum than we do?" She flipped the CommuniClock into the air and let it land on the mattress between us. "My locket, the housekeeping devices, the lights, the boiler. There's a pile of it in the basement. You don't think your nausea could be related?"

"I don't know."

She pulled a locket from the neck of her blouse and released its clasp, dropping the necklace onto the coverlet next to my CommuniClock. "This ruins everything."

I looked from her to the necklace with its twin swallows, and back to her again. I exhaled completely and picked it up.

I came to with a much stronger headache than the last time, and I closed my eyes again almost as soon as I opened them. My stomach roiled, and I ran to the bathroom just in time to lose the contents of my stomach.

When I got back into the room and picked up the box, I was surprised it rattled.

Is the necklace still in there?

But when I opened it, it was not the locket. It was a rock about the size of a walnut, salmon pink streaked with gray.

I don't want to. My brain hurts. Leave me alone.

But I couldn't ignore it.

In fact, edging away from the box made my vertigo even worse, and my stomach clenched its own objection to the spinning room.

I snapped a picture of the rock. And, of course, I picked it up.

CHAPTER

NINETEEN

My brain was splitting with headache.

I was in the upstairs room, Hazel's bedroom, on Hazel's bed. Exactly where I was just a few minutes ago, but now I was alone.

The bitter air made me cough, and coughing hurt. so. badly.

Ow—my head.

"I'd like to know what the devil you thought you were doing," Hazel's father's voice carried from the next room. He wasn't yelling, but each firmly enunciated syllable pounded into my sensitive skull.

He wasn't berating me. My door was closed.

I groaned and rolled to my side, away from the door, but it didn't mute the noise.

"Papa, I'm sorry. We were waiting for the right time to tell you," Laurel said.

I squeezed my forehead with one hand and slipped from the bed in my stocking feet. I crept to the door and pressed my cheek to the cool wood.

"There will never be a correct time to inform me that

my daughter is traipsing around, unsupervised, with some brown boy from an upstart family."

"He's not 'some brown boy.' He's Raúl. And his *upstart father* is your business partner. I thought you'd be happy for us."

"Don't you lie to me. If you'd thought this was good news, you'd not have snuck around with him like some ill-bred minx. This stops right this second, Laurel. You are not to see that boy again."

"That's impossible, Father. The company..."

"There will be no more company gatherings for you. You are to stay away from that boy."

"Daddy, I love him."

"No, you do not. I'll hear no more of this."

"Father—"

"I'll have those vapid books of yours out of your room. If you wish to read, read your Bible. And while you're at that, pray God's forgiveness for your breach of the fifth commandment."

A door closed firmly and his footsteps reverberated as he marched down the hall. The runner on the stairs muffled his footfalls only a little.

I dipped a clean flannel from the dresser-top into the basin of water and pressed the cool cloth to my forehead as I slipped out into the hall.

I turned the knob on the door to the room next to mine, and slipped inside. Laurel was seated on a wicker settee at the foot of her bed, her Bible on the cushion. Her eyes were red-rimmed. She'd abandoned her handkerchiefs, and instead wrung a flannel rag identical to mine in her hands.

I closed the door as noiselessly as I could. She shoved the Bible to the floor and jerked one shoulder, effectively inviting me to sit next to her.

I didn't have a lot of religious convictions, but to leave a book of any kind splayed indelicately on the rug seemed wrong. I picked it up and placed it on her dresser before sitting next to her.

"You shouldn't be up," she said when she saw my own soaked square of flannel. "Your pupils are still enlarged. Lie on my bed."

"I'll be fine," I said. The headache had subsided to a dull thrum, even though only a few minutes had passed.

At least the effects of traveling didn't last long.

I took her hands in mine. "Are you okay?"

She shot me an odd expression, then hung her head. "No. No, I am not. I can't *not* see Raúl. He's asked me to marry him." She extricated a ring from her little cloth bag. It was a smooth, black star sapphire, set in a pale gold band.

"That's beautiful. When did you get that?"

"Today. After you went home ill, I thought Father wouldn't object to Raúl being the one to escort me home. I was clearly wrong on that score." As miserable as she probably had a right to be, her entire countenance brightened when she talked about Raúl.

Was that the way I looked when I thought about Miguel?

She tried the ring on her finger. It was a perfect fit.

"What happened?"

"He kissed me at the gate. Just a brush on my cheek, really, but Father saw. He told me I'm not allowed to see Raúl anymore."

"I heard that last bit and probably everything he said when he was up here."

"I'm going to marry Raúl," she said resolutely.

"Um, okay. You've got lots of time to plan that."

"I don't think I do."

"Look, I'm not trying to be a Negative Nancy, but you're a little young to get married, don't you think?"

"I most certainly am not," she said. "I'll be eighteen in two months. And who is this Nancy?"

"Never mind. It's just an expression. But just because it's legal to get married straight out of high school doesn't mean you should. Are you going to run away? Elope? Don't you want to go to college?"

"I wasn't planning on either of those things. I had no idea Father would be so bigoted. I thought he liked Raúl."

"He may like him fine. Just not for his daughter. Does Raúl know Father disapproves?"

"I don't know."

We lapsed into silence.

"I want you to get a message to Raúl," she said suddenly.

"How am I supposed to do that?"

"Don't pretend you've gotten rid of your Communi-Clock already, nor my locket either. I know you."

I patted the pocket of my skirt. The brick was in there. When I pulled it out, my finger looped around the chain of the locket, so they came out together.

"I told you," she said and sniffed.

I stared wide-eyed at the locket, and the gears whirred, but I didn't launch back to my own house. I flipped it open. Inside was just a mirror.

Why wasn't it sending me back? But then, it was the rock that had brought me here this time.

"Give it to me," she said and plucked it from my palm before I could hand it to her.

She wiped the mirror with her skirt, then pressed her thumb in its center.

"Raúl." She waited. It beeped. "Father knows. It's bad."

She released her hold, and the device clicked six times, then buzzed.

She got up and tucked it in her bedside table.

"I thought you were getting rid of that," I said.

"I can't very well do without it now, can I? I'll not carry it though." She peered through the curtains into the backyard. "Father is discussing my sentencing with Mother in the garden. Do you feel well enough to determine the lay of the land for me?"

"As in eavesdrop?"

"Exactly."

I nodded toward the bedside table.

"Not with that—I said they're outside. Good grief, what has gotten into you? Go out there." She pushed me to the door.

Going outside was far more frightening. I had to pretend to be Hazel, and I've proven to be terrible at that already. I took a deep breath and tried to ease quietly down the stairs. There, on the side table, I spotted my salvation. A little pink-and-gray rock the size of a walnut, sitting atop a silver egg cup.

Gleefully, I grabbed it, expecting the head rush and nausea of returning home. But nothing happened. I rolled it over in my hand.

C'mon, it was the same rock. It had the exact same chevron pattern. Why wouldn't it send me home?

I placed it back on its stand and fell into the nearest chair.

Why didn't the rock work? I couldn't stay here. I didn't belong here.

I stood and stared into the mirror above the entry table. My own face stared back at me. I didn't know if Hazel actually looked like me, or if I only looked like me to myself, but

I didn't like thinking that I actually *did* look like I belonged here.

I tapped the rock again, and when nothing happened, I resigned myself to finding my way through the house.

I stumbled through the kitchen and two red-faced women dropped their meal preparations and stood up straight.

"May we help you, Miss?" the older one in the gray dress asked.

"No," I answered, startled, but not pausing in my trajectory toward the sunshine I could see through the back door. "I'm fine, thank you."

They exchanged a glance. "Are you quite sure, Miss?" the younger one persisted, and moved to follow me.

"Yes, thank you. Sorry to interrupt."

She accepted my dismissal, albeit reluctantly, and it was only when I stepped into the half-inch deep water collected in the laundry porch that I realized I was probably not supposed to go this direction.

I was right, though. There was a screen door to the backyard, and I slipped through it, leaving wet footprints down the back steps.

I peeked out from behind a juniper. Intentional or not, this had been, indeed, the correct way to get here. Immediately on the other side of the row of tall, slim trees—nearest the very one behind which I stood—was the bench on which Laurel's parents were seated. In front of me, and also in the center of their line of vision, was the door where I should have come out, but then they would have seen me, and I wouldn't have been able to listen.

I glanced over my shoulder at the screened-in laundry porch. The young kitchen maid watched me. For a moment

I was afraid she'd give me away, but she sized up the situation, shrugged, and returned to the kitchen.

That was a relief. I was going to have to thank her.

I stood as still as a statue so I could hear what Laurel's parents were saying. The problem was they weren't saying anything. The tension communicated well enough, though, as they sat in stony silence.

Laurel's father—Mr. Scott—spoke first. "Laurel's behavior is unacceptable. We don't know how much damage she's done to her reputation, traipsing around town unsupervised."

"I don't disagree with you on that count, Seathan," Laurel's mother said. Her voice held an edge that communicated she was at least as angry with her husband as she was with her daughter.

"She will not be permitted to see that boy."

"He's not an ideal match, no, but we'll deal with it. My daughter stays here under my supervision while we navigate this circumstance."

"Your inadequate supervision is the reason we have this problem," he barked.

She lowered her voice to barely more than a breath. "Do not insult me because you are angry with our daughter."

"I'm sending her to San Francisco on holiday to my sister's. She can stay there until the situation with that boy has cooled, then she may return. I'll not risk leaving her an opportunity to compromise herself or our reputation."

Laurel's mother's anger elevated her voice to a stage whisper, and when she rose, I had no difficulty hearing her. "If you send her away, I swear I'll never speak another word to you again."

I tucked myself behind the cedar until the screen door creaked and slammed. Laurel's father remained.

After a few minutes he took out a brass brick identical to the one in my pocket. A CommuniClock. He flipped it over to the side with the watch face, cleaned the lens on his pant leg, and pressed his thumb to the glass.

"Deliver to Charlotte—Dear Sister. Sending Laurel for extended holiday. Response requested."

Just like mine, this device clicked six times, then buzzed. He shoved the box into his pocket and stalked into the house through the same door his wife had used.

I weighed my options—go back through the kitchen the way I'd come, or go in the same way Laurel's parents did.

I opted for door number two. After counting out three minutes, I left my hiding spot behind the tree, crossed the courtyard and ducked in through the other back door.

I found myself in a breakfast porch—a sunroom, though it was not particularly sunny with the heavy curtains drawn. I cut through a modest-sized ballroom and found a door that deposited me in the main hallway.

On my way past the entry table, I tapped the rock in the egg holder.

Still nothing happened.

I cursed under my breath, and continued upstairs.

"Dad wants to send you to Aunt Charlotte's," I said, closing Laurel's door behind me.

The color drained from her face. "In California? What did Mother say?"

"That she'd never speak to him again."

"Did that work?"

"I'm pretty sure it didn't." I seated myself next to her again.

"I'll marry him. If I have to do it tonight, I'll marry him." Her eyes shone with fearsome resolve. She was serious. And she was—happy.

"You can't do that," I said. "You're underage."

"After it's done, the only way to undo it would be to make a public spectacle, and Father and Mother care much more about appearances than I do. They'll have no choice but to accept us."

Neither Laurel nor I had heard from Raúl, and her agitation was contagious, so one hour later I was down the block and around the corner, standing on the sidewalk beside my house—Raúl's house. The fence wasn't high. It was laced with grape vines, but it only stood about three feet tall. Raúl's bedroom was the farthest window on the second floor—the one that would be mine someday. Or that was mine now. Just in the future.

I scooped up a handful of gravel, well aware of how strange it was going to look for a young Edwardian lady in a conservative starched blouse and hat to hurl rocks, but I was not nearly as conservative as my clothing would have suggested. I wondered if anyone was, or if they were all just normal teenagers shoved into stuffy old-person clothing.

Using my best pitch, I chucked a few pieces at his windowpane. Two clattered off the porch roof, but one struck its target.

I wound up with another couple of pebbles, but then the curtain moved. I dropped the rocks back into the street and waved to Raúl.

He nodded and disappeared.

A moment later he emerged from the back door of the house. I met him at the gate.

"What's happened?" he asked. "Is Laurel well?"

"Yeah. She's not allowed to leave her room, but she's

well. Her dad—er, Father—is going to send her to California, though. He doesn't trust her to stay away from you." We whispered together as we walked back to the garden where I'd first met him, and where I'd met Laurel. We sat on opposite ends of the bench that faced the carriage house— my bench.

He winced. "Does she want to stay away from me?"

"No," I said. "She wants to marry you."

"Is she ready tonight? I can be ready tonight. I have a cousin who's a minister."

"Where would you go?"

"My cousin is in Leadville. We would have to go there first. My family owns a couple of homesteads in Western Colorado. If we can get to the Grand Valley, we'll open one of those up. I can find work with a cattle or sheep operation out there. My family will help us, I think."

I glanced dubiously at his smooth hands and crisp suit. "You're going to be a cowboy?"

"Don't look at me like that. I'll learn. Or I'll find something with a bookkeeper. I'll figure it out. I have to. I love her."

"Okay. What do you want me to tell her?"

"Tell her to pack light. You can send some things to her later when we're settled—my mother will pay the costs if your father objects. Have her meet me at Union Station at eleven tonight."

We were already speaking quietly, but through the boughs of the giant spruce we saw the figure of a woman— Raúl's mother—move through the backyard.

We went still.

She didn't look our way when she crossed the gap in the vegetation, but slipped silently through the door to the carriage house.

"We need to hurry," Raúl said. "You should go. Talk to Laurel. Tell her my plan. It won't be a debutante's life, but if she's willing to live like a rancher's wife, I can offer her that with me." He rubbed his palms on the thighs of his pants.

"She loves you, Raúl. She'll meet you. I'm certain of it." I got up to leave.

"Not that way—my mother is still in there," he said almost under his breath. "Go this way." He sent me through a gap in the hedge that led me to the sidewalk in front of the house.

I rested my hand on the brick wall as I stepped past it, and for a moment the brick felt squishy, like marshmallow. I sucked in a breath and my vision clarified—all traces of former headache were gone, and the house had done it. Raúl's house. My house. It had fixed my headache.

Something shiny on the path caught my eye. I bent and my fingers recognized it even if I couldn't see the details of it in the moonlight. A tiny brass gear.

I walked, or nearly trotted, the couple of blocks to Hazel's. The sun was setting, and I wondered if I'd been missed. I slipped into the backyard through a gate in the alley, and then apologized my way through the kitchens to the hall and then Laurel's room.

She was lying on her bed staring despondently at the ceiling. She turned her head in my direction when I closed the door. "What did he say?"

I seated myself on the bed next to her and stroked her cheek. "He said it's over and he never wants to see you again."

She jerked upright. "No!"

I pursed my lips and shook my head. "No, you're right. He didn't say that."

She smacked me with a pillow, but she was smiling. "That was wicked. What did he really say?"

I whispered, "He said he loves you and he wants to run away with you tonight."

Her eyes filled with tears, and, before I could stop myself, mine did too. She threw her arms around my neck and we cried and sniffed while I filled her in with whispered details.

At half past ten I was under the covers in Laurel's room. My pillows—er, Hazel's pillows—were artfully arranged in a human shape under the coverlet in that room, but her parents were less likely to check in on me. I had little doubt they'd be keeping an eye on Laurel tonight.

I'd helped her out a side door with her one small bag ten minutes ago, and now I lay in her sheets with my curls, which looked similar enough to hers, fanned out over her pillow.

Our elaborate ruse was for Mother's benefit, as Father wasn't even home. After his disagreement with Laurel's mother he'd gone to his club.

I'd only just drifted off when I was startled awake. I had no awareness of what had roused me, but all the hairs on my body stood on end.

I eased the sheets back and slipped out of bed. The house was middle-of-the-night silent, even though I was certain it was not yet midnight. The stairs didn't even creak under my weight as I snuck down to the foyer.

I picked up the rock for what must have been the tenth time that day, but again nothing happened.

Moonlight filtered through the sheers and illuminated the house with a bluish hue. I couldn't help myself. I stepped into the parlour just so I could feel the thick, soft wool of the Persian carpet on my bare feet. In all my museum and antique store scouring, I'd never seen one so fine.

But the unsettled sensation kept me from really enjoying it.

I wanted to go home.

I walked a slow circle of the room, inspecting antique end tables, which were probably still brand new and not antiques at all, and browsed a row of small leather-bound volumes—Virgil, Homer, Dante, and some others in French. I picked up one of the French ones to see if there were any illustrations inside.

I sensed something behind me and turned just as the front door was thrown open. Laurel stood in the doorway, her hair wild.

"Laurel, what's wrong? What are you doing here?" I dropped the book onto the sofa and hurried to her.

She stood still in the doorway, a delirious look about her. I grabbed her by the shoulders and shook her a little. "Laurel!"

Her mouth opened, a sob escaped, and she crumpled in my arms. She tried to speak, but she was completely unintelligible as sobs wracked her body. She wiped the tears and snot from her face with the back of her hand. "He tried to kill him, Hazel. Father tried to kill Raúl."

"What?" I stumbled under her weight.

We dropped to our knees, but in the process, I bumped the sideboard with my shoulder.

The egg cup tipped over, and the rock fell off the edge.

Without thinking, my hand shot out, and I caught it.

TWENTY

When the world steadied, I was in my room—my empty room in the upstairs of the old empty house—curled in fetal position next to the box. My headache was back and much worse, and I clutched at my splitting skull with both hands.

Groaning, I rolled to my elbows and knees, keeping my head tucked to block the light from my eyes. Movement exacerbated my nausea and made me dry heave, and dry heaving made my head pound.

It was me now wiping the tears and snot away.

I tipped over to my side on the hardwood, squeezed my eyes closed, and willed the pain to stop. But it followed even as sleep claimed me.

———

Night time. Corseted waist. Gravel street.

I exhaled in irritation, smoothed the creases from my skirt, and raised my chin.

I took three steps across the gravel street when a horn blared. I whipped my head toward the sound that wasn't supposed to be in this dream.

I didn't have time to register the car's distance from me, blinded by its headlights. I instinctively dove back toward the sidewalk, knowing I wouldn't get out of the way in time.

And even though I was sure I must have shouted, I couldn't hear it over the car's horn and the distant wail of a siren.

———

I woke to the buzz of my cell phone in the pocket of my shorts. I was still groggy, but thankfully the headache was gone. So, evidently, was the sun. Only the fading purple twilight illuminated my empty room.

I pulled out my phone. 8:31.

Omigod, Dad was going to kill me.

I had two texts from Miguel, but I called my dad first.

"Where are you?" he answered, without even saying hello.

"I'm at the house still."

"Still? What on earth are you doing?"

"I wasn't feeling well, so I laid down. I fell asleep. I'm sorry, I didn't mean to make you worry."

"And you didn't notice any calls? Okay. Close up and go home."

"Go? Where are you?"

"The Boettcher fundraiser."

"Oh yeah. Okay. I'll be out of here in a minute."

"Love you," he said.

"Love you too."

I ended the call and checked my texts.

Miguel 7:28: I can't stop thinking about you.

Miguel 8:31: Just walked past your house. Are you there? Your truck's outside, but no answer at the door.

My heart fluttered.

Me 8:32: I am, but I'm leaving now.

I sat back and pulled my knees to my chest. I needed time to think. About Laurel. About Raúl. About why those charms appeared and disappeared, and why I went in the first place. And why it made me so sick.

Right now, I was just so damned glad to be back.

I flipped open the lid of the box again.

Oh no.

There was a paper inside.

No, I was not doing it. I was not going back. I couldn't.

My stomach knotted up even at the suggestion. And that last headache had been crippling.

It could stay there until tomorrow—I didn't care. I wasn't touching it.

The small browned page looked like a recipe, but it wasn't in English. It wasn't Spanish either. It was from the *curandera* journal—the page was torn on one side and there was the same printed rose in the corner.

I snapped a picture of it with my phone. It was face up, and curly scrawl filled the whole page. I flipped the box and let the paper flutter to the floor, which it did, but it landed with the same side facing up.

I sighed and scooted away from it.

I didn't have the time nor the strength.

I tapped my palms on the floorboards at my sides, then just turned away from it. I pushed myself to my feet and closed the bedroom door behind me.

In the bucket at the top of the stairs sat my tool pouch.

I glanced back to the closed door of my room. *I should leave well enough alone. It could wait until tomorrow.*

But those needle-nose pliers would do the trick.

I pushed my bedroom door open again, toolbelt in hand. Using the rubberized handle of a screwdriver I pinned the page to the floor and scraped at the corner until it puckered, so I could grab it with the pliers and flip it.

Success.

I snapped a picture of the back, and forwarded both shots to Miguel with the message, "Do you know what this is?"

I left the box and the page on the floor, but I tucked the tools back into their pouch.

But what if it can't wait until tomorrow?

I messed with the doorknob and avoided looking at the paper. I looped the toolbelt over the knob, pulled it off, hung it again, shifted my weight, messed with the strap some more. Then shot an accusing glance at the paper.

"He tried to kill him, Hazel. Father tried to kill Raúl."

This might have been an emergency. What if it couldn't wait?

I trudged three paces, hating the idea, but knowing it's the right thing.

I squeezed my eyes shut, lay down on my back so at

least I wouldn't fall, and touched my fingertips to the paper.

Nothing happened.

I sat up and tapped at it repeatedly. *Just what the hell was going on? I thought there was a system here.*

I turned the page over in my hands. Notes were scrawled in the margins in the same ink, but a seemingly more rushed penmanship. I couldn't make out a single word on the page—just the numerals in the list on the front.

I returned the sheet to the box and closed the lid.

Just when I thought I had the idea of how this worked.

I popped the lid open again, and, like a cheesy magic trick, the paper was gone.

No, what the actual ef?

I shoved the box away, sending it skittering across the wood of the floor—very uncharacteristic treatment of an antique on my part. It bumped to a stop against the baseboard and I scrambled to my feet and sailed out of the room, slamming my bedroom door behind me.

I was about to go through the front door when I remembered I haven't locked up.

I tossed my hoodie and keys on the entry bench and made a rapid circuit of the downstairs, closing windows and checking door locks.

I've got to do something about the nasty vomit taste in my mouth.

At the bathroom sink I splashed water on my face and brushed my teeth as best I could with my finger. My eyes were a little red, but I don't look too horrible.

The doorbell chimed.

If it wasn't Miguel, I wasn't answering it.

It was him though. And Tito and Javier.

"Hey," I said. I waved to his friends, but my attention zeroed in on Miguel.

A grin spread across his face, and *was that a blush?* He leaned his skateboard against the side of the house. "I didn't think you'd be here this late."

"Neither did I."

"Listen, we're headed to the skate park. It's open 'til eleven. Do you want to come? Jenny's meeting us too." He took my hand, tugged me down from the step, and looped his arm around my waist.

"I can't," I said, but I hooked my thumb on the pocket of his shorts. "I've got to get back home. My dad is already worried."

His smile evaporated like a kid who'd dropped his lollipop.

"Have fun though." I gave the tip of his nose a playful tap.

"I knew it was a long shot, but I thought I'd try." Completely unconcerned that his friends were right there, he planted a soft kiss on my mouth, then released my hand and backed down the steps to where Tito and Javier waited on the walk.

"Good to see you guys," I said, and waved.

I turned to go back into the house, but the door was closed.

Shit! How did that happen?

Goosebumps popped up all over my skin.

I tried the handle, and it was locked. My keys were still on the bench in the entryway.

"Dammit."

Miguel and his friends stopped at the gate.

"I was standing right here. When did that close? I'm locked out, and my car keys are in there."

They set their boards down. Javier said, "No big deal. There's probably a window open or something."

"I don't think so," I said. "I just locked everything. Let me call my dad."

The guys circled the house anyway. After they found no way in, they perched on the edge of the porch. I appreciated that they were keeping an eye on me. I felt safe enough in this neighborhood, but no one wanted to sit outside in the dark, alone.

Dad picked up, and I explained what happened. "Okay." He sighed. "I can come get you."

Miguel mouthed, "Ask if you can come with us."

"What time is your thing supposed to be over?" I asked.

"Midnight, why?"

"I can just hang out with Miguel and his friends 'til you're done there."

His tone turned sharp. "What are Miguel and his friends doing at the house at a quarter of nine?"

"They stopped by to ask me if I wanted to go to the skate park with them."

"Kassandra, you're not inspiring my confidence right now, and I'm really not okay with my teenage daughter wandering around Denver at night."

"I'll be totally safe—I'm with three guys." The boys heard this and flexed their muscles like body builders.

Morons.

"That does not make me feel any better," Dad said.

"Dad, you know Miguel. He's a good kid."

He mumbled something that I didn't quite catch.

"Come on, Dad. It's an unforeseen turn of events. This makes sense."

He exhaled into the receiver. "I don't like this, Kassandra, but I trust you. Don't give me reason not to, okay?"

"I won't, Dad."

"Be on our porch by eleven so you don't get into city curfew trouble."

"Yes, sir."

"I love you, kid."

"I love you too, Dad." We hung up. "All right, I can go. I don't have my board though."

Miguel blinked twice. "You have a board." It was a statement, not a question.

"Yeah, of course, but it's at home. Natural-wood deck, Bones bearings—"

"I love you. Will you marry me?" Miguel grabbed me by the waist, bending me backward to kiss me like in a movie.

"How does he always get the good ones when I've got all this charm and good looks?" Javier asked.

"It's because girls can tell what a *pendejo* you are, *güey*," Tito said.

TWENTY-ONE

"You guys, I want a Slurpee," Javier announced as we passed a 7-Eleven. Without waiting for agreement, he veered toward the door. "You want anything?" he called over his shoulder.

"I could go for some chips. We'll come with you," Miguel said. We walked in step with his arm around my waist. Whenever I'd seen couples walking together like this I thought it looked like it'd be awkward, but it wasn't really. At least not with him.

"Birthday cake," Tito said, tossing a pack of Hostess cupcakes to Miguel.

"Aw, yeah!" Javier grabbed a couple more. "Let's celebrate."

"Whose birthday is it?" I asked Miguel.

"Mine," he said, his face turning pink. "Tomorrow."

"Oh my gosh, why didn't you tell me?"

"Because it's not a big deal."

"It's a big deal," Javier said. "Birthdays should always be a big deal. And you're eighteen, so you can officially do whatever you want."

"Right," Miguel said. "Which is exactly what I already do."

As the boys picked out their snacks, I browsed the chocolate selection and grabbed a pack of Rolos to take to the counter.

"My treat, Princess," Miguel said, taking the candy from me and placing it on the counter with his.

"No, Miguel. It's your birthday. I'm buying." I already had my money in my hand.

"My birthday is tomorrow, not today. Are you really going to try to deny me the chance to declare my love for you with ninety-nine cents?"

"Fine," I said. "But only ninety-nine cents' worth of love. I wouldn't know what to do if you loved me a whole dollar's worth."

A middle-aged man with a curly red beard waited impatiently behind us in line while Miguel dug his cash from his wallet. He didn't bother whispering when he said to the woman next to him, "This place is full of Mexicans now." His tone of voice made it clear he did *not* view that as a good thing.

My mouth dropped open in shock. I'd never heard an adult behave so rudely.

Javier, Tito, and Miguel ignored him, but I could see Miguel's jaw muscles tighten.

Javier, who'd already paid, took a long drink from his Slurpee and used his nail to scratch a gummy patch of adhesive residue from the counter.

"They come here with their twelve kids, and hard-working taxpayers have to foot the bill to school 'em. I just don't think it's America's responsibility to educate them ignorant foreigners," he continued and took a step closer.

Tito stepped out of his way and looked at the door, like he was imagining himself on the other side of it.

Miguel picked up his change, slapped his palm on the counter, and turned to the man. "I agree with you there," he said. "Let me pause for a moment to educate an ignorant foreigner for free. My family's lived in this square mile since before Colorado was a state. You, sir, are the interloper, but I'll leave you to look that up since a moment with a dictionary might improve *your* English."

He jammed his receipt in his pocket, grabbed our Dr. Pepper bottles, and turned away. "Ignorant foreigner." He took my hand.

I grabbed our bag just before he pulled me out of the store.

Tito and Javier followed closely behind, and the door closed on the stunned silence of the entire store.

"Nicely done," Javier said.

I agreed. No one could have put that man in his place quite the way Miguel had. I ambled along beside them without speaking.

Something about that exchange bothered me. At first I thought it was because I'd never had racism directed at me or my friends, but there was something else, too. It was something Miguel had said.

We crossed the grass and sat on top of the picnic table in the bright glow of the skate park lights.

"I'm an interloper," I said.

Javier and Miguel looked at me.

"I'm an interloper," I repeated. "If not for me and my dad, you'd have a shot at getting your family's house back."

Javier said, "If not for you and your dad, Miguel's family wouldn't have a house to try to get back."

"I wasn't talking about all *güeros*, Kaz," Miguel said.

He was talking into his bag of Hot Cheetos. "And, yeah, you're an interloper. But you're lovable so you're forgiven."

"I'm as new as you are," Tito said, low enough that only I could hear.

When Miguel jumped down from the table Tito said, "What's that ribbon hanging from your pocket?"

Miguel tugged on it. "What? My keys?"

He showed the charm, its broken thread dangling from the loop.

Tito's eyes widened. "Your *mal de ojo* broke? *Vato*, you got to get a new one. It stopped a curse."

"Not you too, Tito." Miguel turned away.

"No, man. I'm serious." Tito looked to Javier for backup, but Javier shrugged. Tito shook his head and said, "You tell 'Uela your thread broke. She can bless it and tie a new string."

"I don't believe in curses, man," Miguel said.

"*Amigo*," Tito said. "Curses don't care whether you believe in them or not."

<hr>

Jenny arrived, looking gorgeous in her all-black ensemble of miniskirt, lace top, and Chucks. Neither Tito nor Javier knew what to do with themselves.

We hung out until quarter of eleven. The guys seemed pretty pleased to have an audience to appreciate their hard-practiced skate tricks, and they took turns lending us their boards so Jenny and I never had to spectate very long.

And I had to admit it was pretty fun showing off my kickflip.

As we squeezed through the gate to leave, Javier and Miguel high-fived the police officer there.

"How's it going, Officer Mike?" Javier said.

"Good, good. It's been nice and quiet tonight," he said. "Have a good one."

"You too, man."

"You guys know the cops?" I asked.

"He used to be our school officer. He's a good guy," Javier said.

"Do you guys want a ride?" Jenny asked, jingling the keys of her Beetle.

Miguel and I exchanged a glance. "You know," he said, "it's a beautiful night. I think we'll walk."

He squeezed my hand, and I blushed.

"Tito?" she asked.

"Yes, please."

She hit the unlock button, and Tito opened the driver's side door for her.

Javier shook his head and hopped on his board to skate along beside us.

"You mad, bro?" Miguel asked.

"Naw. Some girls can't handle this much appeal. Like looking right at the sun, you know?"

"Glad your self-confidence is intact," Miguel said.

I couldn't help but notice how different the city felt at night. Not just different from its daytime ambiance, but also from the suburbs I was used to.

A siren ululated in the distance. Cars rushed past on a semi-busy boulevard. Javier's skateboard wheels clacked over each sidewalk crack. And it wasn't even dark. I mean, the sky was, but streetlights hung like miniature suns every half block.

Crickets chirped in the brush beside the walk. They fell

silent at our approach only to take up again after we'd passed, but their song was familiar enough.

At 38th, Javier waved and ducked through the gate to his home behind the *taquería*. Miguel and I walked the additional blocks to Grove.

He and I sat on the edge of the porch to wait for my dad. I brought up the *curandera* recipe page on my phone and asked him what he thought of it. We killed almost an hour trying to figure out what it meant, which led him to explain some of his grandmother's astrological lore to me.

Miguel pointed out constellations in the barely visible pinpricks of light in the night sky. The corner streetlight was out, but the milky haze of the city lights made it hard to see any but the brightest stars.

"I always look for Orion," I said. "It's usually easy to spot three stars in a row and the fourth at a right angle to it." I got up and turned a circle in the yard, but I didn't see it.

"Orion is a wintertime constellation," Miguel said. "You won't find him up there tonight. I prefer the lady anyway." He took my hand and led me across the yard and into the quiet street so the trees didn't block our view.

He pointed to a cluster of stars that formed a W. "Cassiopeia. She's more beautiful than the sea nymphs, and she knows it. Still, I can respect a woman with attitude." That last part he said with his gaze fixed, not on the stars, but on me. He cocked a half grin and brushed a stray lock of hair from my face. Our lips met, right there in the middle of the street.

I was so caught up that at first I didn't notice the sirens —the ubiquitous sirens of the city—until something clicked.

My dream.

I pulled back from Miguel and looked over his shoulder toward 38th, just in time to see a car, its headlights off, skid around the corner and head right for us.

The horn blared.

I squeaked and reacted, whipping Miguel past me by his shirtsleeve, propelling him ahead. We leapt across the sidewalk and up the embankment. The car swerved, and one— two— three police cars flew around the corner after it, their lights and sirens blaring.

The dark car veered as it accelerated down our street, but the first police cruiser clipped its bumper. Both cars spun, sending the dark one into the light pole and a piece of plastic shrapnel hurtled through the air at us. We jumped out of the way, and it ricocheted off a nearby tree.

The other two police cruisers screeched to a halt next to the then-immobilized dark car and the officers jumped out, guns drawn.

"We shouldn't be here," Miguel said.

"Across the street from my house?" I asked.

"No." He pulled me up the steps onto a neighbor's porch. "Anywhere guns are." He dropped my hand to vault over the low brick wall on the far side of the porch and ducked down on the other side of a brick exterior wall, against the backyard fence.

I followed a half step behind.

From our relatively sheltered position we gripped each other's hands and listened while the arrest went down.

"That was scary-close," I said. "We almost got taken out —twice! Happy birthday to you, right?"

In the dim light I saw a strange expression cross his face, and he looked at me with—if I'd had to label the expression, it would have been mistrust.

He nodded. "Yeah, almost killed on my eighteenth

birthday. What'll my grandmother have to say about that? She'd call it a curse."

"Curse?"

"I come from a long line of single mothers. The men of my family die young."

"My family too. If my dad makes it into his sixties he'll be the oldest of his line. It's not so much a curse as it is poor food choices and heart disease."

"No, I mean *really* young. Like before twenty."

"That is young. What happened to them?"

"My dad was killed in Iraq. He got my mom pregnant after basic and before deployment. The others—sickness, accidents, I don't know."

"That's scary—in light of what we just experienced. You take care of yourself, huh, Miguel?" I put my head on his shoulder and nuzzled his neck.

"There's nothing to worry about. Their deaths had nothing in common. Curses are just what the old women called it when they were trying to explain unfortunate occurrences."

"You're the one who brought it up."

"Because it's what 'Uela would say. It's just not how real life works."

The yelling on the street had quieted down. The police seemed to have the situation under control.

A week ago, I'd have been more inclined to scoff at the idea of a curse, but a week ago I'd never been to 1911, so I cuddled myself closer into Miguel's embrace, inhaled his soapy boy smell, and worried enough for the both of us.

After a few minutes he released me and crept to the front of the house to gauge the activity on the street.

"They've got the guy in cuffs on the ground. Guns

holstered. Let's cross over to your porch. Your Dad is going to be pissed if he shows up and we're not there."

"Worried more like it. He's going to see that mess."

We linked hands again and moved down to the sidewalk, then across the street and up to my porch. One of the officers glanced up at us, but they were too busy to care about enforcing a city curfew.

We settled back into the shadows of my porch just as Dad arrived.

TWENTY-TWO

I was too tired to drive by the time Dad showed up, so I just grabbed my keys and slumped into the passenger seat. Miguel climbed in the back, and I was sure Dad must've dropped him off at his house, but I didn't remember any of that. After I fastened my seatbelt, the motion of the car knocked me out.

The room was dimly lit, but my eyes were already adjusted to the light, or lack of it.

I lay on my back, my head and shoulders propped up on soft pillows—bolsters under my knees and ankles. It might have been a comfortable position if my body didn't hurt so much. My left side ached as though my ribs were broken, and I couldn't move my left leg. My right side felt like rug burn from my knee to my face.

"Ugh. Mommy—" I groaned, and then remembered I didn't have a mom anymore.

A cool hand touched my forehead. *"Hush, mijo. Cálmate,"* a woman said.

Mijo?

She moved into my line of vision.

Not my mother. Raúl's. But her touch was no less comforting.

She was short and of stocky build, and her wavy black hair was down past the tips of her fingers. She was beautiful, with a broad face and high cheekbones, and her eyes curved gracefully upward at their outer edges.

Her belly was round. She was pregnant. Very pregnant.

She touched a wet cloth to my face, right in the spot where it hurt. I flinched away instinctively, but she persisted, and the pain evaporated with the moisture from her cloth.

She dipped the cloth again, then touched it to my shoulders. She moved the sheet the way a masseuse would, protecting my modesty, but addressing the scrapes on my side, hip, and leg. The pain disappeared from every place she touched with the wet cloth.

I looked down at my exposed chest—I was as flat as a board. As in even more so than normal. I wasn't me at all. I was a dude.

I sucked in a breath, and the woman pressed her hand to my forehead. "Shh."

She continued soaking my wounds, then returned the cloth to the bowl of ointment, and lit what looked like a skinny bunch of weeds. In the sudden flare of light, I could see more of the room. Four stone walls. A door. No windows.

The smoke from her smoldering bouquet drifted lazily around the space, and she waved her smudge around me, and then around the entire room. She paused in each corner, but I couldn't understand what she was muttering.

A few feet away from me a fire burned in a small iron stove.

Like the one in Kaz's basement.

No—I was Kaz. My basement.

My basement. Who was Kaz?

The woman blew out the flame and placed her cool hand on my forehead. She waved the smoking bouquet over me a second time. The smoke smelled sweet, like incense, and made my eyelids heavy, but didn't necessarily make me feel sleepy. I just wanted to close my eyes. The pain in my left side was too strong for me to sleep.

She returned the smudge stick to an enormous seashell and placed it on the other side of the fire, adjusting its position twice before she seemed satisfied with it.

She took a flat, hot stone from beside the fire and pressed it into my side.

I yelped and tried to scoot away, but she pressed harder. The heat of the stone burned my skin, but the rib pain diminished.

"*Otra vez*," she said, her voice like sandpaper. Deep, melodious sandpaper.

She took another flat stone from beside the fire and pressed it to my leg. Again, the skin seared under the heat of the rock, but the other pain was sucked into that heat. Given the choice of the two, I was glad to take the burns. She didn't give me the choice anyway.

She used a palm-sized stone mortar and pestle to mash something and spread the still-chunky, oily substance onto the burns with her fingertips. It smelled like lavender. The burning didn't go away, but it didn't make it worse either.

"*Descansa ahora, mijito.*" She wrung out her wet cloth,

folded it in half, and placed it over my eyes. *"Tú debes descansar en sanar."* I heard her blow out the candle.

In the darkness my breath seemed louder. Oddly, I couldn't hear hers. I blinked my eyes and my lashes caught on the cloth. It moved a little.

I alternated squeezing my eyes closed and raising my eyebrows until the cloth obstructing my vision shifted enough for me to see. All of that facial movement pulled on the abraded skin of my cheek and made it burn again, but it was nothing compared to how much I hurt just a few minutes ago.

Madre.

She was not my *madre.* She was Raúl's *madre.*

Madre.

She had her back to me. She tended the fire in the center of the room. A breeze, probably the updraft from the fire, played at the ends of her hair.

She kneeled next to the flame with a small leather book open in her left hand. I could hear her murmuring, but couldn't make out the words. They weren't in English, and they weren't in Spanish either.

She fed what was left of her flower smudge into the flames, just a few stems at a time. When they were gone, the flames had grown into a respectable blaze, the tongues of fire licking the air at knee height.

She knelt next to a basket, from which she extricated three jars, the largest a quart Mason jar, and the smallest the size of a baby food container. She didn't measure the contents, or maybe they'd been portioned when they were placed in the jars. She unscrewed the top from each, and swaying while she chanted, she poured the contents into the fire.

She took a wad of bloodied gauze from the basket. The

blood was still crimson even in the dim light, so it couldn't be old. It was probably mine.

She rose to the balls of her feet, but remained squatted. She crossed herself three times and spoke the first words I understood, "Seathan Scott, you hurt my son. Your hate will come back on you and rain with a mother's fury."

She cast the gauze into the flame, and a scream rattled the small room and everything in it.

It was mine.

TWENTY-THREE

The nightmare shifted, and I was a small child carried by my dad. Except that I was not dreaming anymore. I wasn't little, but he was carrying me just like he used to.

He deposited me on my bed and covered me with my afghan, snuck out, and closed my door behind him.

I blinked in the darkness of my room, sweaty curls sticking to the back of my neck. I was glad for the interruption, and a little afraid I'd slip into the same dream if I fell back to sleep.

Even though my body didn't hurt any longer, my whole being remembered a blinding excruciation as though it really happened to me.

Everything hurt, and my limbs prickled with renewed circulation. I rolled to my side and wiggled my way under the comforter, but couldn't shake the anxiety left from the dream.

I buried my face in my pillow, but the sleepiness from the moment before had evaporated. Instead, my nerves thrummed with adrenaline, as though I'd been running for my own life, and when I closed my eyes I saw the dim room with its bare stone walls, smoky sage incense, and pain.

I vaulted out of bed with no plan. I couldn't stay there a second longer—as though it were the source of the nightmare I'd had when I wasn't even in my own bed.

I sank to the floor and crossed my legs under me, but the metal eyes of my work boots dug into the sides of my bare legs. Absently I fumbled at the laces, pulling them off the hooks without even untying them, then tossing the grubby things into the corner by the door.

I wrapped my arms around my legs and rested my chin on my knees.

"*Your hate will come back on you,*" and then pain.

All the pain from before the healing, compounded and magnified to the brink of what a body could bear, which, in reflection, was more than I would have thought I could take without going into shock. But then, it wasn't exactly me taking it. And it hadn't been Hazel. I had been Raúl. And we were both in his head at the same time.

'Uela was right. There had been a curse—I was there when Raúl's mother had cast it upon Laurel's dad.

So, had it been it Raúl who had been in pain, or the Hazel part of me? It definitely wasn't the *me* part of me because I was fine.

My body shivered its objection to the memory.

I leaned over, clicked my lamp on, and grabbed a small notebook from my bedside table. Almost everything in my room was packed away in the boxes stacked next to the closet. We couldn't move into the new house until the kitchen was finished, at least another week, but I wanted to be ready.

"*Three jars—red powder, dark mulch-like stuff.*"

I tapped my lip with my pen. I never saw what was in

the medium-sized jar. I skipped a line and filled in the rest of what I remembered.

"A smudge that smelled a little off. Like sage mixed with something else. Something sour, with flat scale-like leaves the size of my thumbnail."

"Bloody bandages—Raúl's?"

I clicked my pen on and off against my thigh, channeling my nervous energy into repetitive motion. It dissipated only a little.

That's all I could remember, but it felt like I was forgetting something.

Not English. Not Spanish.

"'Seathan Scott...Your hate will come back on you'"

She'd cursed Laurel and Hazel's dad. What if that cursed Laurel and Hazel as collateral damage? I could have felt Hazel's pain in the nightmare. Maybe I was in Raúl's body because something happened to Hazel. And Laurel.

A sense of dread crept over my skin, raising goosebumps on my flesh while my heart sank. Laurel was my friend and my sister. And Hazel was, well, she was me.

I'd plugged their names into search engines and gotten no real results, but I should have used the library's database. I didn't know anything about them.

What if they were dead?

But then I felt stupid. Of course they were dead. They were teenagers over a hundred years ago. They were definitely dead by now.

But that's not the same as dying because I didn't do something I was supposed to do.

I clicked my pen a few more times, then twirled it in my fingers when another thought occurred to me—*What if they grew up and had kids? Where would they be? Their kids or grandkids could still be alive.*

I scrawled across the page—*"Look up Laurel and Hazel Scott."*

But not right then. Right then I was tired again. And sad.

I dropped my notebook and pen into the nightstand drawer and shucked my shorts. When I climbed back under my covers and hugged my pillow for comfort, I was still wearing my sweaty tank top, and I was too sleepy to care.

———

Night time. Corseted waist. Gravel street.

I exhaled in irritation, smoothed the creases from my skirt, and raised my chin.

I can't go into the street. No, don't cross the street!

My legs initiated the step without my consent.

Gravel crunched under my boot, but the sound was a different kind of crunch. A creak, like metal under strain.

I looked up as the awning pulled away from the store-front's façade.

I leapt away from it.

The car horn blared, and with it, a siren.

———

The next morning Dad drove us back to the house.

"How'd you sleep, kid?"

"Pretty well, I guess. I had trouble falling back to sleep after we got home, but after that—" I shook my head. "Sleep of the dead." I did feel rested, though, like I'd already knocked back a cup or three of coffee, but without the jitters.

"Good, 'cause I want to talk about last night." He was at a stoplight, so he leveled his gaze at me.

My heart rate jumped, and I knew this wasn't going to be good.

"Why don't you go ahead and explain how events transpired."

"Where do you want me to start?"

"Start with the part where you didn't answer your phone when I called."

I pressed the back of my skull into the headrest behind me and closed my eyes. I wasn't good at lying to my dad—it wasn't something I'd made much of a habit of doing, mostly because I sucked at it.

Which he knew. And which was probably exactly the reason he was asking me. So he'd know if I was lying.

But I couldn't really lead with, *So our house sometimes sends me back in time, and it totally gives me a tummy ache.*

"I didn't answer because I fell asleep. I wasn't feeling well."

"You took a nap at the house? Where? On the floor?"

"Yeah. In my room upstairs."

"Kazoo, that's not safe. What were you thinking?" The light changed and he turned his attention back to driving as he moved around a truck shifting through its bouncy lower gears.

I shot him a confused look. "How is that not safe? Sleeping in my own room in our house? Is it somehow less safe because there's no furniture?"

"No, noodle brain. Overworking yourself and passing out without telling anyone you're ill is what's dangerous." He was silent for a moment. I didn't even need to look over. I knew he was working his jaw while he was thinking.

I rapped my fingertips on the armrest. "Go ahead, Dad. What else is bothering you?"

"The boys," he said. "I don't like that they were at the house when I wasn't."

Oops. Guess I shouldn't tell him about Tito and Javier helping us paint the second floor then, what with that having been unsupervised.

"And I don't like you wandering around town at night. And I *really* didn't like coming around the corner and seeing all those police cars in front of our house. I should have just left the fundraiser and gone to pick you up right away."

"Dad, why? That doesn't even make sense. I'm fine. Those cops would have been there either way—they weren't there for us. Relax."

"I mean that I was too permissive last night, and I don't intend to make a pattern of it."

"Okay." I let a long breath out of my nose and nodded. "I'm sorry my bonehead mistakes made you worry."

He took his hand from the shifter and mussed my hair. "Eh." He paused to sigh. "It's not just that that makes me worry, kid. We dads worry about our teenage daughters. It's what we do."

We rattled along a few more blocks, and when I glanced at him his jaw was still working.

"Yes?" I asked.

He cast me another sidelong glance. "What's going on between you and Miguel Montaño?"

My cheeks grew hot and I immediately turned my focus into an intense interest in my boots while I tried to figure out how to answer.

"Um, we hang out." I trailed off.

He cut to the chase. "Is he your boyfriend?"

"We haven't actually defined the relationship *per se*."

"But you've hooked up?"

"Oh my God, Dad, no!" I covered my face with my hands. "No, Dad. We're, like, kind of dating. *Hooking up* means having sex. We're not hooking up."

He rolled his eyes. "I'm pretty sure the term is a bit more ambiguous than that. Do you kiss him?"

I pulled my splayed fingers down my face until they just covered my open mouth. "I can't believe I'm having this conversation with my dad," I said to the dashboard. "Yes. I've kissed him. Yep."

"Do you see how that's a bit of a game-changer for me? I mean, I like the boy. But there are some things you and I are going to need to talk about, so I'll know you're safe, and I won't have to kill the lad."

Kill the lad. My memory jogged to last night. Raúl. What had Seathan Scott done to Raúl?

My thumb pressed into my rib cage, testing to see if it hurt. It didn't.

"Kazoo?"

"Dad, do we have to do this right now? This is so embarrassing." We were only a couple of blocks from the house, but I was afraid he'd get on a roll and wouldn't let it go.

"No, of course not. I can bring it up some other time." His whiskers twitched into a smile. "Preferably when your friends are around."

"Oh, you think you're so funny." I smiled in spite of myself.

TWENTY-FOUR

I slapped a coat of gripper primer onto the freshly stripped cabinets in the kitchen and had time for the first thin coat of bright white paint. Since it'd need time to dry completely, I cleaned my brushes and told Dad I was off to the library again.

"Which one?" he asked.

"Central. I want the Western History department."

"That's my little nerd." He shook his head and resumed routing a design onto the board clamped to his sawhorses. "Stop and get me another pack of one-hundred-grit sandpaper for the orbital on your way home."

"Yeah." I watched transfixed for a moment as the maple sheet became a cabinet door. Four more just like it leaned next to their older cousins, waiting for the paint that would make them identical.

"Hey, I left some flooring samples in the kitchen. Would you have a look at them when you get a chance?" he asked as I turned to leave.

I called over my shoulder, "I already have. I put them in order, best to worst, and I threw away all the samples of linoleum pretending to be stone or wood." I raised an eyebrow. "I kinda think if you want stone, get stone. Don't get an imposter."

He nodded his head, frowning a little, then raised his gaze. "You've got a good point. Go ahead and leave your favorite on the windowsill and toss the others. I trust your judgment. I want to get it ordered."

"Done and done," I said, feeling pretty happy to find Dad so agreeable on the matter.

"Oh, hey. Could you pick up your grandma at two? I've got a code inspector supposed to stop by."

Highway driving the twenty-five miles out to the airport. "Yeah. No big deal." At least I'd see Grandma today. I still had plenty of time for search-engine stalking.

I grabbed my bag, the notebook inside of it, on my way. I hesitated for a moment in the entry. I hadn't been upstairs at all today. I hadn't even looked at the box, let alone checked inside it, but I was not doing it right now. I wanted to know what happened to Laurel and Raúl, but I wasn't signing up for vertigo. Besides, if those events took place in the past, then it didn't matter when I went back. It was the past. What was the rush?

In the meantime, I was going to find out what happened to them the modern way—I was going to look them up on the souped-up, genealogy-equipped internet of the library system.

I locked the front door behind me.

Not a single cloud interrupted an expanse of sky the color of cornflowers, but that lack of atmosphere at elevation made the sunlight blinding, even at ten in the morning.

The construction fence had been hauled away, so the yard felt bigger and brighter without it. Some puny marigolds had pushed their way through the leaf litter and were defending their territory beside the walk. I pushed some of the leaves back from their bases to get them some room and made a mental note to take a rake to the yard as soon as possible so the surviving vegetation might stand a chance.

When I turned back toward my truck, standing next to the passenger side door was Miguel's 'Uela, with three shopping bags in her grip and a mañanita shawl draped across her shoulders as though it weren't already ninety degrees.

I blinked my surprise. *"Buenos días, Señora."*

She nodded and pressed her lips into a thin line. Her lively dark gaze paralyzed me. She was not here by coincidence, and I doubted it was a casual social call.

"Would you like a ride? I'm headed to the library, but your house is in the same direction."

"Walking is good for the body and the soul. Nobody walks enough. Not the young. Not the old," she said.

I looked pointedly at her bags. "I'm sure you're right," I said, "but it's pretty warm and your groceries are getting hot." I unlocked the passenger side door and swung it wide.

She nodded once and let me take her bags and help her in, as though she had never intended or suggested she would do otherwise.

By the time I got around the truck and into my seat, she had her seat belt on, her hands folded in her lap, and the three bags, their handles knotted, arranged on the floorboard beside her feet.

I pumped the gas pedal to start the engine. As I pulled out, I noticed she was looking at the clay charm and ribbon she gave me, which I wore on my right wrist.

"This symbol," I said, "it's on one of the porch railings at my house. What's it mean?"

"It is a blessing," she said, barely raising her voice loudly enough to be heard over the chugging of the little truck's engine. "The symbol is Mexican, but the spoken words are Ute."

"Oh. Do you speak Ute?"

"Not as much as I used to," she said. "Turn right."

"Here?" I asked, surprised. It wasn't the way to her house, but I slowed and flipped my turn signal manually for the tailgating minivan behind me. I'd been meaning to get the flasher fixed, but I kept forgetting.

"Stop here and park," she said, indicating a space in front of the botanica, a small herbalist store Jenny liked so much.

Without explanation she opened the door and slid out, leaving her bags behind. I took this as an indication that she'd be right back, so I left the engine and the air conditioning running and tapped my thumbs on the bottom of the steering wheel.

The herbalist was in a little brick midcentury-modern addition to an older commercial property with second-floor apartments. On the other side, a mansion at least as old as our house sprouted determinedly from behind another 1950s blond-brick addition. Glass block windows. Classy. Like the marijuana dispensary housed there now.

Three minutes passed and 'Uela emerged. She climbed back into the truck. *Climbed* was probably not actually the right word since my truck was no taller than a normal car. She deftly tapped the leftmost button on the radio panel, silencing it.

From her skirt pocket, she produced a tiny charm of

pressed tin shaped like a pair of closely-set eyes. A *milagro* —like the charms I'd seen nailed to saints' altars.

She threaded a slim red ribbon through it, removed a tiny vial from the same pocket and let three drops fall onto the charm and its ribbon, cupped in the center of her palm.

"Give me your wrist," she said.

I did. The one nearest her was the one with her clay charm on it. She tied the new charm next to the *mal de ojo*.

"This is to help with your Sight," she said.

"My sight? Is there something wrong with my eyes?" I didn't wear contacts.

She looked at me like I was stupid, and we both knew which kind of sight she was talking about.

"This—" she placed the tiny vial into my palm and curled my fingers around it "—is for your head. Put a drop under your nose if you get a headache. If the pain is very intense, burn a few drops and breathe the smoke. It will be white. You may cough, but you must trust that it is good for you."

"Okay." I turned the vial over. It was unmarked except for a tiny sticker on top of the cap, on which was written in ballpoint pen—*copal*.

I tucked the vial in my pocket and reached for the gear shift, but she intercepted my hand.

"I need to read my mother's journal," she said.

"*Your* mother's journal?"

"Miguel showed me. You sent him a picture. I need to see it. Can you go back and get it?"

"No," I stammered. "I can't. I would, but it's gone."

Her face registered disbelief. "You've lost it?" And then horror. "It was stolen?"

"No, ma'am." I shook my head emphatically. "They—

the things I find in the house—they disappear. That's why I take pictures."

Her expression relaxed, and she accepted my explanation as though it were rational.

"Okay," she said. She turned away slightly and nodded several times as though agreeing with someone I couldn't hear. "Okay, but you have photographs. Let me see the photographs then."

"Yeah, sure." I pulled my phone out of my back pocket and called up the photo app.

As a precaution, before handing it to her I hit "Share" and sent them to myself in an email. I didn't have a reason to think she'd delete them, but just in case.

I handed the phone to her and showed her how to toggle between the two pictures and to zoom in and out.

She enlarged the photo to its maximum size and scrolled back and forth like a pro. She was better with technology than I would have given her credit for, and I noticed also that she held the phone like a normal person, not at arm's length, the way Dad did when he didn't have his reading glasses on.

She scanned down the page shaking her head more emphatically the further she read.

Staring at her while she read felt awkward, so I turned my attention to the new charm on my wrist. It was kind of sharp—I was going to need to be careful with it. I took the little brass gear from my pocket, untied the string, threaded the gear onto it and retied the strand.

'Uela gasped and dropped the phone into her lap as though it had burned her, and I thought maybe I'd done something wrong, but she wasn't paying any attention to what I'd been doing. She covered her mouth with her fingertips and shook her head. "This is not prayer and healing. *Brujería*."

"What's *brujería*?"

"The work of a witch. I cannot participate. It is forbidden. I am a healer." She gazed out the passenger side window, and I saw tears welling in her eyes.

"Participate in what?" I was sitting sideways now on the seat, facing her.

She took my hand in both of hers and shifted toward me. My phone slid off her lap and bounced off the parking brake between the bucket seats.

Neither of us reached for it.

"You have to undo Miguel's curse."

"Okay," I said slowly. My mouth went dry. I was still looking at 'Uela, but my mind called up that little room with its smoke and pain. "How am I supposed to do that?"

"You have to reverse the *hechizo*. I can write the instructions for you, but a healer can never venture into dark arts. The consequences would be dire." Her rasp dropped to a near-whisper. "My mother would have known."

"'Uela?" I said.

"Yes."

"Is the house cursed?"

"No. Not cursed. Blessed," she said. "Only we are cursed. Miguel, especially. You can help us. Help him."

"All right." I said automatically, not knowing what I was agreeing to.

That must have been what she wanted to hear. She dropped my hand and turned to face front again. She put on her seatbelt, which I took as my cue to move along, but first I pulled my phone from under my seat and returned it to the safety of my pocket.

I looked over my shoulder and threw the truck into reverse.

"Okay," I said, in answer to nothing.

She didn't speak again for the rest of the ride.

———

Miguel was at work, so I didn't see him when I deposited her grocery sacks on the counter.

"Okay, then, I'll talk to you later, I guess," I said.

She dropped the notepad and pencil she was holding onto the heavy wooden table in her kitchen. "Where are you going?"

"The library." We'd already covered this, but she was old, so whatever.

"No," she said. "You need to stay here. You don't have time."

"Time for what?"

"You need to undo the *mal hechizo*."

"What, like now? This is something I can just do right now?" I pulled out a chair and sat down.

"You will know how after I translate it. Give me five minutes. Go get the leather journals from the shelf in *la sala*, please."

"Yes, ma'am." My heavy chair squealed against the linoleum when I scooted it back. I should grab some felt casters from the garage and fix that for her next time I was here, before the substantial chairs wrecked the floor.

I collected the six small leather volumes from the curio cabinet and tucked them safely into the crook of my arm. I lingered for a moment longer to run my thumb over the carved mahogany leaves. A century of lovingly applied furniture wax had accumulated in the crevices, but the skilled craftsmanship that went into the piece was undeniable.

I wished I could do that, but woodworking, particularly the fine detail of cabinetmaking, was not my strong suit. Dad had the steady hand and patience for it, but I was better with plaster and paint.

I returned to the kitchen table with the books and arranged them on their backs in a neat row according to numbers inked on the faces of each.

'Uela was still working intently, and, to my surprise, she had already copied nearly the whole front side of the notepaper.

She was printing her translation using perfect, tiny lettering, like a draftsman's or an engineer's.

> 3 herb sticks:
> desert sage, for purification and spiritual
>   safety
> juniper, to open the eyes
> *Euphorbia montana*—miner's bane spurge,
>   to activate intention
> earth—from Seathan's home
> Buena Vista salt
> pinewood
> tokens—Seathan's and Raúl's

"What's that mean?" I asked. "Tokens?"

"Something that belongs to the person." She selected one of the leather books, undid the strap, and flipped it open to a chart hand-drawn on the last page. "Particularly an article used daily. It's best to use a sample from the individual's person."

"Clothes and jewelry?" I asked.

"They would do, but hair or nails would be better. Blood is best. Less powerful means less predictable results. That is more dangerous."

"How do you know all this if you're not allowed to do it?"

"The principles are the same for healing." She jotted notations next to two of the ingredients and turned both papers over to write the instructions.

I sat quietly, listening to the tapping of her pen as she worked. Finally she pushed the paper across the table's surface toward me.

"My grandmother made a terrible mistake," she said, her hand still covering the page. "She cursed a man, but the Guides punished her anger by turning the curse back on her. It's why the boys in my family never grow old. They pay for her error. It's why Miguel, too, will die."

I winced. "Will? Don't you mean *might*? I mean, not if we undo it, right? And you know how." He couldn't die. He was too young.

"We are racing with time, and the curse is already in effect. Miguel is in danger every second we delay. Will you do it?" she asked.

"Repeat the spell?"

"Yes."

"Okay."

"Not *okay*. I want your word. Yes or no?"

"Yes, ma'am."

She took her palm from the page and pointed to marks she'd made next to the ingredient list. "I made notes as to where to find the herbs. Go now. And, *Avellana*, do not tell anyone of this. Invoking favors is dangerous work, and the spirits you will beseech are not friendly ones. No one should be involved who doesn't have to be."

"Okay—yes."

"Hear me." She held both of my forearms in her vise-like grip, and her cloudless cocoa eyes impressed the gravity of her meaning into mine. "It is not safe. Burn this when you are finished, and remove it from your phone. Words are powerful in all their manifestations." She turned me toward the door and pressed the center of my back.

"Yes, ma'am."

At the stoop she tapped me again on my back, and when I turned, she held up a finger indicating that I should wait a moment. She poured water from a small pitcher into the ornately painted bowl, dipped her fingers into the water, blessed me in Spanish, and closed the door behind me.

I typed *avellana* into translate.

It meant hazelnut.

She'd called me Hazel.

I didn't know where to go. I wanted to go to the library and look up Laurel and Hazel Scott, but 'Uela said this was more important. Miguel was more important. If 'Uela was right, I had to get on this hex reversal immediately.

I unfolded the copy of 'Uela's counter-spell. A token from Seathan Scott? How the hell was I supposed to come up with that? Nothing that'd been in the box had been his. Even if it had been, those things disappeared after I touched them.

I was going to have to find a way to get something of his and bring it back. I needed to go to the house. I needed to go to 1911 and be back in time to pick up Grandma.

Relieved to have a plan, even if it was determined by default, I started the truck and steered my way back to the main thoroughfare.

Clark's Hardware was on my way home, so I stopped to grab Dad's sanding disks there. Plus, it came with the added convenience of a Miguel sighting.

The place was dead on a Wednesday morning, so the

bored girl at the desk welcomed me and, before the bell had finished announcing my arrival, asked if she could help me find anything. Sandpaper was on aisle seven. A guy stocking gloves and gardening gear at the end of aisle three paused in his work to ask me the same question.

"Nope. I'm good. Aisle seven," I said.

I couldn't imagine how they could afford so many employees. The customer service was nice though, if a little eager.

Sandpaper—100 grit. Check. I tucked two five-packs under my arm and went looking for Miguel. Bosses weren't usually pleased when employees' friends came in when they were on the clock, and I didn't want to get him into trouble—but navigating the gauntlet of bored-yet-helpful people was tricky. I eschewed the main aisle and made for the rear of the store.

As luck would have it, the next employee I saw was Miguel. His back was to me, and he was at the far end of that last aisle stocking cleaning solvents from a pallet.

I tried to think of something clever to call out as he expertly heaved gallon-and-a-half jugs onto the shelf. His muscles rippled under his shirt while he worked, and I wasn't sure I could think clearly enough to flirt. I was putting a little swagger in my walk when my saucy smile froze on my face.

Plaster dust sprinkled from anchors that were supposed to be embedded in the wall. They weren't.

The braces twisted with the weight of the shrink-wrapped back stock on the top shelf, exacerbated by the seismic thuds of new product on the bottom shelves.

Miguel didn't see it.

Dropping the sandpaper, I yelled, "Omigod, Miguel, MOVE!" and launched myself at him, closing the twenty-foot distance in probably two strides, just as the shelf buckled.

I instinctively hit him in the side with my shoulder, like a trained football player, and shoved him back through the swinging door to the Employees Only storeroom.

He managed a surprised, "Wha—?"

The creak and crash of the shelf behind me answered his question—and it triggered a switch in my brain.

I heard that last night. In my dream. The awning.

"Oh my God, Kaz. That was close." He threaded his fingers into my hair and pulled me into a bear hug, which was kind of uncomfortable since it put my weight on my now-bruised hip and the unforgiving concrete floor.

I didn't care. I was just glad he was okay.

He finally released me and helped me to my feet, but kept a supportive arm around my waist. He seemed so calm, but I was shaking.

Every employee in the store rushed to the scene, including Bud, the assistant manager on duty, who breathed a visible sigh of relief when he spotted Miguel with me in the doorway.

"Is everyone okay? Wow, that could have been really bad. What happened?"

No one answered. I was the only one who'd seen.

"The shelving anchors failed. The whole thing buckled." I picked my way around the debris so I could indicate the detachment points. When I turned back to Miguel, I saw the stack of buckets that had been immediately next to where he had been working just moments before. A shelf had cleaved through the top ones.

And since the buckets were unavailable, when I turned away, I had no place to throw up but the floor.

TWENTY-SIX

I had to bully my way to the curb at Arrivals if I didn't want to circle again and again in the off chance that the stars would align in my favor and a space would open up. I nosed into a spot under the Frontier sign, and Grandma materialized at my door before I could set the parking brake.

She heaved her rolling bag over the side rail into the truck bed. She clearly didn't need my help.

I leaned over and unlocked the door.

"Hi there, baby girl." She slid in and kissed my cheek.

"Hey, Gram."

"What's the matter?"

"What do you mean?"

"You're perturbed. What's going on?"

I pulled out, and a Mini took my place before I was completely clear of it. "Grandma, you've been in my car for maybe twenty seconds. How would you know if I'm perturbed? Put your seat belt on, please."

She did. "I know my granddaughter. Don't change the subject."

I gave her a half smile and glanced over my shoulder before merging onto the beltway around the terminal. I got away with silence until the airport exit, but then she cleared her throat.

"Maybe it's just dealing with the highway. I hate driving on the highway."

"Kassandra," she warned.

"I don't know where to start," I said.

"Pick a spot. You can circle around to herd the rest of the details in later."

"Okay," I said, but then I was quiet for several more beats. "I'm worried about one of my friends. A boy. Bad things keep happening to him."

"What kind of bad things?"

"Like he was almost run over by a car last night, and today a shelf of really heavy stuff at his work fell over and completely obliterated the spot where he'd been standing."

Grandma whistled through her teeth. "Two close calls. Bad luck. But your...friend...he's okay?"

"Yeah, he didn't get hurt."

She tapped a tiny fingernail on the console between us. "But you didn't say you were traumatized. You said you were worried. Why are you worried?"

Nailed it. *How had she she done that?*

I gritted my teeth, then just blurt it out. "His *abuela* thinks he's cursed."

She blinked twice. "Cursed. Do *you* think there's a curse?"

I puffed my cheeks as I exhaled, and nodded once. "Yes. Yes, I do."

She nodded once also. "This is new. I see you're wearing a *mal de ojo* and a *milagro*. I think your world view has changed since I've seen you last."

"Yeah," I said. "Probably a bit."

"Then you need to tell me more about this curse and this boy."

We approached the house from the south. I tucked into the neighborhood a few blocks early and drove a couple of blocks out of my way to show Grandma some of the more interesting historic homes—the 8,500 square foot Lumber Baron Mansion, with its oddly modern weathervane artistic installation; a whole block of high-style Queen Annes; and two turreted gothics designed by architect William Lang.

"That one's ours." I waved my finger in the general direction while sweeping my little truck into a U-turn to park on our side of the street.

"Well, would you look at that?" Grandma stared up through her window, and for the first time I see it as it is now, not as it was less than a week before. The old siding and faux-rock veneer have been removed, the bricks sealed, and mortar repointed—all by Dad's teacher friends. The porch was still crooked, and the woodwork needed paint, but anyone could see it now—this house would be beautiful. Grandma deadpanned, "But I worry about the two of you having enough space. A three-story mansion? Was that necessary?"

"Yeah, right? I told Dad we were going to rattle around. You're going to have to move in with us just to take up space." I slammed my door and walked around to get Grandma's for her.

"Whew." She put her hand to her forehead as I helped her out. "This thin air is dizzying."

"It is." I pulled a water bottle from my bag and handed it to her. "Guzzle some. You don't want to get altitude sickness." I moved her suitcase into the cab of the truck and locked the doors.

Dad appeared on the porch. "Mom! I'm glad you could come. How was your flight?"

Grandma paused for another dizzy spell on her way into the house.

Dad escorted her to our one camp chair in the kitchen, where she sat with a fan blowing on her while I brewed her a cup of coffee.

"I'm sorry, it's not like me to be so afflicted. Must be getting old."

"Don't be silly, Grandma. Young people get altitude sickness too." But she did look old. Her cheeks looked sunken, and there were dark circles under her eyes. She seemed to have aged ten years in the five days since I'd seen her.

I touched my fingers to her forehead. Her temperature was fine, and her color seemed normal.

She took a long sip from her coffee. "Hmm?" she asked. "What did you say, dear?"

"Young people get altitude sickness too."

"No, after that."

I shook my head. "That's all I said."

She frowned, shrugged, and downed the rest of the cup like it wasn't hot.

"How does that not burn your mouth?" Dad asked, as amazed as I was.

"I'm not in the habit of waiting for my coffee to get cold

before I drink it." She rose and moved to wash the cup, but I took it.

"Would you like another?"

"No, dear. One should be enough." She patted my arm, and there was a moment when her pleasant expression faltered and she leaned momentarily on me.

"Gram, sit down."

"No, I'll be fine, dear. Jet lag. Let's have a tour. What have you two done?"

"Mom, she's right. You should probably lie down. Kaz, could you do one more coat on the cabinets? I'm at a stopping point. I can take Mom back to the other house."

She released her grip on my arm and headed to the hallway without us. "You may take me home, and I promise I'll lie down and rest, but I'm here right now, and I'm not leaving until I see this house."

"Yes, ma'am." He shook his head and shrugged.

I tagged along on the tour, and Dad led Grandma around the first floor, pointing out various architectural features and explaining what we still had yet to do. After we climbed the stairs Dad pushed me to the front, so I showed Grandma the guest room and its closet first.

The latch in the closet pulled easily now, and I'd installed a cabinet pull so it could be closed again. When the door swung open to reveal the narrow, curved stairs to the kitchen, Grandma was suitably impressed.

"A secret passage to the kitchen in the closet of the guest bedroom?" Grandma asked. "Perfect for midnight snacking. How considerate of you."

"Isn't it?" I said. "We'll move our stuff next week, so stick around and you can get started. We offer first-class hospitality here—turn down service, a mint on your pillow, and secret passages. Try to find a better place to stay in Denver. Just try."

"It's classic too, isn't it?" she said. "I could swear I've seen a stairway exactly like it in a movie or something. That patch of crumbling plaster is utterly quaint."

"I had that wall distressed just for you, Gram. It's shabby chic."

"Quite."

Grandma praised my paint choice and the new closet woodwork in my room, and hummed her approval at appropriate intervals for the rest of the tour, then kissed me on the forehead and told me she was proud of me before she left.

"Couple hours?" Dad said to me. "Home around eight or so?"

"Sounds about right."

"Have you eaten dinner?"

"I had a Power Bar."

"Okay. I'll make a pasta. You need real food. You're still growing."

"You think?" I squared my shoulders and stretched myself to my maximum height, which made me almost as tall as his chin. "It's hard enough to buy jeans as it is, but it'll make me a blocker to be reckoned with." I pantomimed smacking a volleyball into the ground.

I saw them out the door and transferred Grandma's bag from my truck to Dad's car. As soon as they were gone I closed and locked the front door behind me, then took the stairs two at a time to the second floor.

I knew how I was going to get a token from Seathan Scott. If I could go back to Hazel's house and take something of his and hide it someplace, like bury it in the yard or something, when I came back to the present it would still be there for me.

I didn't have time for sickness, but I didn't have a choice.

I lifted the folded drop cloth from the top of the box, dropped to my knees, took a deep breath, and lifted.

It was empty.

"Are you kidding me?" My voice echoed in my empty room. "How am I supposed to get a token if there's nothing to send me back?"

I closed the box, gave it a little shake, and opened it again.

Still empty.

I slammed the lid and rolled my eyes, not that anyone was present to witness my exasperation. I raked my splayed fingers over my scalp, jumped to my feet, and paced the room.

With no other ideas, I cast the drop cloth back over the box and stormed downstairs to paint the cabinets like Dad told me to.

TWENTY-SEVEN

I padded into the kitchen to find Grandma in an apron, up to her elbows in flour. Dad sipped coffee at the table in the corner and read the paper.

"What are you doing?" I squinted at the brightness of the room with the shades all pulled up.

"Baking bread."

"At seven a.m.?"

She raised an eyebrow at me. "It *is* something that's traditionally done in the small hours of the morning. Are you chastising me for getting a late start?" She plopped the ball of dough into a waiting mixing bowl. "It's only six in California."

"We are going over to the house this morning, right?" I retrieved a bowl to load with cereal.

"Of course, dear," she said. "That's why we need the bread." She pulled a fresh dish cloth from the drawer, draped it over the bowl, and tucked the whole thing into an oversized tote balanced on one of the chairs.

She gathered the broom from the pantry and leaned it by her tote.

"There's already a broom at the house," I said through my mouthful of Cocoa Puffs.

"That nylon thing?" she said. "I saw it. I'm taking this one. I'll need two towels also, please."

"We've also got a laundry basket of clean towels at the other house," Dad said.

Grandma washed her hands and wiped the counter. "Okay, I'm ready. Are you two ready?"

I was only five bites into my breakfast. I hurriedly shoveled in two more spoons full, but then could hardly chew.

"No, Mom. Sit down and have a cup of coffee."

The corners of her mouth turned down for a fraction of a second, but she appeared to think this not so terrible an idea. She settled into the chair next to mine and poured a serving of fragrant black liquid from the carafe. She poured a second cup, just like the first, added cream to them both, and slid one to me.

"Thanks."

"Don't mention it."

I sipped a bit of the milk from my bowl to make it easier to fish out the last bites of cereal. "What've you got in the bag?"

She smiled with a stage-worthy false innocence. "Cleaning supplies."

"Because the solvents we have there already are in some way inadequate?" I asked.

"I have—" She pursed her lips and glanced to the side. Her eyebrows arched her emphasis when her gaze returned to me and she said, "preferences." She knocked back her coffee and sat the empty cup down.

Dad folded his paper and topped off his cup—black. "Did you two sleep okay?"

I shrugged. The same dream on replay. It wasn't worth mentioning.

City street at night. Broken awning. Car horn. And this time, the store exploded into flames. A cheerful nighttime experience.

Grandma, though, furrowed her brow. "It's the oddest thing. I woke up with a terrible fright, but I can't remember a thing about it. Maybe it's the sleeping tablet. I thought I'd outgrown night terrors."

"People outgrow nightmares?" I asked.

Dad shrugged. "Not me. I still get 'em. Especially in August before school starts again."

"Maybe I've had them all along, and it's my memory that's failed." She tapped her empty cup. "Aren't you two finished yet?"

Dad drained his cup. "She'll give us no peace."

I dumped my still-scalding coffee into a to-go tumbler and got a move on.

I knew I'd have errands to run today, so Dad and I took separate cars. Grandma rode with me, which put a damper on my plans to sit in the driveway for a few minutes texting Miguel.

Instead, I drove carefully, following Dad at a respectable distance. Even though it was rush hour, CDOT had lanes closed for resurfacing, so I had to drive past my normal turn.

"Oh, let's stop there!" Grandma put her hand on my arm and pointed past me.

"Where? The botanica?" Was there some old-lady

attraction to that place? "Grandma, they're not going to be open yet. It's seven thirty."

"They're open. I just saw someone go in. Look, there's a parking space right out front."

It was totally weird that every time an old lady got in my car, that's where she wanted me to take her.

I flicked my semi-functional turn signal three times and took advantage of the traffic stopped at the light, switched lanes, and cut across the double yellow line into the parking spot Grandma indicated. Breaking laws for my grandmother.

"Come on," she said before I even pulled the parking brake, and, for the second time in less than twenty-four hours, an old lady slipped out of my passenger seat and, without waiting for me, headed to the door of the herbalist.

I cut the engine and leaned across to lock her door behind her, then trotted after her. She was already inside.

I didn't know what I'd been expecting. A greenhouse? A witches' dark apothecary? What I actually found was a spacious store, brightly lit and tidily organized. Grandma was chatting happily in Spanish with a middle-aged man behind the counter.

I stood back a few paces and pulled up the picture of 'Uela's list on my phone. She had two items marked for here —desert sage and Buena Vista salt.

I sidled up to Grandma, and she introduced me, still in rapid-fire Spanish. I blinked and smiled awkwardly while I tried to follow, but only caught a quarter of the words.

He placed several items on the counter in front of her. A burlap sack smelling strongly of lavender, three vials of oil, and four railroad spikes.

I glanced between the giant nails and Grandma with an expression that very clearly requested an explanation, but

Grandma ignored me and handed the man two crisp twenties, and he bagged her purchases in a brown sack. She turned to leave, but I said, "*Espere.* Um, do you speak English?"

He smiled. "What can I do for you?"

I turned my phone back on to look at the list. "Do you have desert sage? And, um, Buena Vista salt?"

His salt-and-pepper brows pulled together to form an almost continuous line. "I think so. The sage, yes. Let me check on the salt. How much do you need?"

Shit. I didn't know. Enough to throw into a fire? "A tablespoon?"

His expression changed from one of jovial humor to something more cautiously skeptical. "One moment."

"Is that locally sourced?" Grandmother interjected before he disappeared through the curtained doorway.

"Yes, ma'am. A hundred fifty miles away or so."

"I'll take some of that too. One and a half pounds should be sufficient." To me she said, "I've got this."

"No, Grandma. I brought money."

The man nodded and disappeared. When he returned, I consulted my list again. Two items were unmarked.

"Do you have juniper?"

"Oil?" he asks.

"No, like branches of it."

"It grows everywhere. I don't sell it. You can cut it and dry it yourself."

"Yeah, I guess so." My face reddened, but I took another shot. "What about Miners' Bane Spurge? Have you got any of that?"

He frowned and shook his head. "Never heard of it."

"Oh. Okay." I tried the scientific name. "*Euphorbia montana?*"

He shook his head again.

"Okay. Just these then. Thank you." I pulled out a twenty of my own, but Grandma brushed it away and paid.

The bell jingled again on our way out, and Grandma said over the noise of the traffic, "What on earth is Miners' Bane Spurge?"

"I have no idea." I unlocked her door and walked around to mine.

"Then why do you need it? Are you smudging juniper for Sight or protection?" She grilled me as soon as I opened my door.

"What are you talking about?"

"Does this have to do with your friend?"

"Yes," I answered without hesitation.

"Okay," she said, but she watched me for several seconds before looking away.

I parked behind Dad's car and carried in our purchases. Dad had brought the cleaning supplies with him. The moment I could do so politely I ran up the stairs to my room and opened the box.

It was still empty.

That totally killed my plan of stealing Seathan's token and burying it in his yard.

Dirt, though. I needed some dirt.

I hopped down the steps and out the front door without saying where I was headed, then realized I didn't have a container for it.

Groaning, I returned to the house and slipped back in as soundlessly as I could, but there was no avoiding Grandma. She'd opened two windows in the kitchen, and she was working her way through the dining room and living room, hoisting open any of the sashes that weren't painted shut.

I grabbed a Ziploc bag from the pantry, where our

supplies had been shoved since the kitchen cabinets were out of commission.

I couldn't help but be seen going out the door now, so I went ahead and paused to ask, "You know the swamp cooler circulates best if only the window farthest from it is open, right? Because the air gets sucked out of the nearest opening—"

"I've heard that, yes," she said, but pushed the next sash all the way up anyway.

"Okay." I didn't make her explain, and when I slipped out the front door, she didn't ask where I was going.

I knew I was in full view of the very windows she was standing at as I jogged down Grove Street, past a duplex, two very old turreted Victorians, and several bungalows.

I was a little winded by the time I stopped at the eight-foot iron fence, which had withstood the trials of the century with remarkable aplomb, a few wrought-iron points missing, but still staunchly straight and strong.

A sign on the walkway gate read, "Law Offices of Carlino Sandoval & Associates, LLC."

Carlino Sandoval and his associates must not be doing a very brisk trade, if the weeds growing around the property and the missing shingles on the roof and tower were any indication.

The gate was locked with a chain and a padlock.

"Walk-in appointments not accepted?" I said.

There was no soil reachable by this gate, but a double-car-width gate spanned a packed-dirt drive along the edge of the property. I trotted over to it and clawed some clay from the tire ruts and dumped it into my bag.

I hoped this counted as Seathan Scott's dirt, and I wasn't inadvertently screwing over Carlino Sandoval and Associates. I didn't even know them. I pocketed the bag and ran back to my house, enjoying the stretch of my legs in the not-too-hot morning air. I'd not been getting enough exercise since we'd started this project. Unless heavy lifting counted, which of course it did. But running. I'd not done nearly enough running.

I slowed to a walk when I came to our neighbor's house and plopped down on the curb in the shadow of their fence line. I could hear Dad's power tools whirring in the garage behind the house, but I wasn't visible to either him or the house from here.

They had an overgrown juniper bush, and I snapped a few small sprigs from it, reaching for the dry sections just past the green front layer. I stuck them into the pocket of my flannel shirt and pulled out my phone.

08:14 ME: Hey, how're you doing?
08:15 MIGUEL: I'm okay, thanks to you. How many times are you going to save my ass?
08:15 ME: How many times are you going to need it saved?
08:16 MIGUEL: Fate's taken two good shots at me and I hope she's given up. I've exceeded my near-death allotment for the week, yeah?
08:17 ME: Your grandma doesn't think so.

My phone was silent for three full minutes.

08:20 MIGUEL: I don't want to believe in that garbage.
08:21 ME: I'm worried about you.
08:21 MIGUEL: Don't you start too. Please.
08:22 ME: I'm sorry. Not trying to irritate you.

This time when the phone was silent, I slipped it into

my pocket, stood, stretched my legs, and made for the front door.

Of course that was when my phone buzzed again.

08:25 MIGUEL: Can I stop by and see you after work? 1:15?
08:25 ME: Yep. I'll be here.

This time I held the phone for a full two minutes before putting it back in my pocket.

TWENTY-EIGHT

Grandma was humming somewhere in the house, but I climbed two flights of stairs before I found her on her hands and knees scrubbing the floor in the attic, murmuring as she worked.

"Grandma, just use a mop and vinegar water. I don't think the hardwood can handle as much attention as you're giving it."

"It needs to—this is important. I'll add a layer of linseed when I'm finished. Instead of giving your opinion, how about you grab a towel and help? It'll go faster, and you should learn."

"I'm pretty sure I know how to scrub a floor, Grandma."

"But do you know how to bless a home?"

That caught my attention, and I asked in a much more encouraging tone. "Blessing a home?"

She stilled her brush for a moment and fixed her gaze on me. Her face showed concern, and she asked quietly, "What's happened to you? You used to dismiss mysticism of any kind."

Instead of answering, I hopped back down the stairs, calling over my shoulder, "Just a sec. I'll be right back."

I dug for a moment through the various supplies and gear we'd piled in the laundry room and returned with two pairs of contractor-grade knee pads and a clean hand towel.

Grandma's face softened into a smile when I handed her a set. "Bless you, sweet child."

In moments we'd put them on and were kneeling side by side.

"You're feeling better then?" I asked. "No dizziness?"

"Just the tiniest bit. Not like yesterday."

"Are you sure you should be working this hard?"

"Dear, when you get to be my age, discomfort becomes the norm. If I stopped for every little affliction, I'd never get anything done."

I didn't have a response for that. "What is this we're using?"

"This is salt and lavender. I can keep scrubbing the floors with this, and you can wipe it with lemon vinegar. When it dries we'll go over it with a fresh coat of linseed oil."

"Okay." I grabbed the spray bottle of vinegar from the rim of her bucket and started at the stairs.

"No, dear. Wipe this direction, always toward the exit, finishing at the back door of the house."

"Why?" I asked. "I mean, not that it's harder, but why do you care which direction I wipe it?"

"Because we're pushing the bad intentions away, and we don't want to dump them on your neighbors."

"We have neighbors behind our house too, you know."

"Yes, dear, but there's an alley."

"The alley's even narrower than the street in the front.

Are our bad intentions really just looking for someone to afflict?"

"There's my little cynic. I was wondering where she'd gone." Grandma patted my hand with her yellow-glove-covered one. "They aren't our intentions. They're negative energies that have accumulated. We'll cleanse the house, bless it, and you and your father will be healthier and happier as a result."

"Grandma, anything the salt doesn't kill, the vinegar will. That's not mysticism—that's microbiology."

"What makes you think mysticism is independent from the sciences? Willow bark and spiraea will help a headache. It's magic. It's also aspirin."

"Okay." We worked with surprising speed, and within the hour were in the laundry room, scrubbing the linoleum and wiping it all the way to the back door.

"Take your shoes off," Grandma said, and we padded back over the clean floors in our socks, and with two of us working, made short work of slathering all three floors with linseed oil.

"Why does this smell so good?" I asked.

"It's a little strong, isn't it? I poured rosemary oil into it. That way you won't have nightmares."

I jerked my gaze to her face. "Who said I have nightmares?"

"You did, this morning. And also when I read your cards. They were right about the lovers, too, yes?"

I didn't reply.

"That was exhausting," Grandma said. She peeled off her gloves and dropped them into the supply bucket. "Is this the cellar?" She opened a door.

"Yep."

"Let's have a look then."

The steps were uneven. Dad and I would have to replace the treads and maybe even the stringers, but we'd had other priorities. After my last time jump as Raúl, I'd not been very keen on doing anything down here.

Grandma halted at the bottom step, and I ran into her.

"This is—interesting," she said.

Miguel and I had hauled the garbage up to the dumpster, so the space was clear but for a long wooden table, two folding chairs, and the squat wood-burning stove along the right-hand wall.

"Now, why do you suppose there'd be a little fireplace down here?" she asked.

"To heat the space, I'd guess." I didn't tell her about how I saw it being used. I pointed to the modern furnace and water heater in the other corner. "Those haven't been here very long."

"Sure, I've just not heard of anyone needing to heat the cellar. They were supposed to be cold—people didn't have refrigerators. Say, there's your coal chute."

I was getting antsy. I didn't like it down here. "Yeah, hey, are you thirsty? Let's go up and get some lemonade."

She gave me an odd look. "Sure. Why don't you pour us a glass and let's catch some breezes outside?"

The table out back was sitting in full sun, so we opted for the plastic chairs on the crooked front porch.

"What's this? From your admirer?"

There was a wildflower bouquet in a glass vase beside the door. The card tucked in amongst the leaves contained no To/From information, just the words *Euphorbia Montana* handwritten in the perfect print of a draftsman or engineer.

"Miners' bane," I said. From 'Uela.

"They're pretty."

She was right. Tiny round five-petaled white flowers

clustered at the end of pointy-leaved stalks, and there must have been twenty of them. It looked like a presentable bouquet, not the wad of herbs I expected it actually represented.

"Why don't you put them on the sideboard, dear? Brighten things up in there with some cheer."

I turned to do as she instructed, but she gasped and sat up suddenly.

"What? What's wrong, Grandma?" I plunked the flowers down and was at her side in a moment. Had she had a vision?

"Sorry, I didn't mean to frighten you. I only just remembered I wanted to put the bread in the oven. I was just so drained, it slipped my mind."

"Oh. Okay. I can put it in."

"Would you? It's rising in the pantry yet."

"Of course."

I headed inside with the heavy vase of blossoms, which I'd never place directly upon the gorgeous wood of the sideboard. It had made it this long without water stains, and I'd not be the one to ruin it. I placed a doubled paper plate between the glass and the wood to serve as a coaster and plucked a handful of sprigs from the bouquet to dry them with the juniper.

The skin on my neck prickled and, without looking directly at it, I was very aware of the beveled glass that once showed me the fully decorated parlour of the past. But it felt like I was being stared at. Or like when two people pass in the aisles of a grocery store and are aware of each other and take in each other's attributes, without being so impolite as to actually look up and watch each other openly.

Only the other one *was* openly watching. When I raised

my gaze, I saw my own reflection and that of the room behind me, nothing amiss, in the mirror.

I shivered and ordered my tensed muscles to relax.

We hadn't moved in yet, and I was practically dealing with PTSD associations in each room of the house.

I clenched my jaw and turned away from the glass, but its attention remained until I crossed the threshold to the kitchen.

I flicked the switch on the giant 1940s range I'd convinced Dad was too cool to replace, and the oven lit up.

The bread dough sat in a loaf pan under a dishcloth and beside a stash of chips, sodas, and snack foods on the pantry shelf. Even through the window, it was just a room with shelves.

While I waited for the oven to preheat, I assembled a Lunchable-like snack plate of cold cuts, cheeses, and crackers. For good measure I added a pile of grapes and almonds, then a puddle of some fancy horseradish mustard. I doubted Grandma'd had anything to eat since breakfast.

Before taking the tray out with me, I dug through my bag for my notebook and retrieved 'Uela's list. I leaned on my elbows at the counter while I scanned through it— desert sage, juniper, and miner's bane spurge—check. I just needed to research the process itself, though I'd witnessed that once through Raúl's eyes.

Earth from Seathan's home—check.

Buena Vista salt—check.

Pinewood—I glanced out the window at the stack of firewood beside the fence. Who knew what kind of wood it was? Could have been pine, but could just as likely have been spruce, cottonwood, aspen, or any number of burnable species. Then I noticed the two-by-four scraps scattered on the ground around Dad's sawhorses. Bingo.

Pinewood—check.

Tokens—Seathan's and Raúl's—I still don't know what the hell I was supposed to do about that. I'd had an excellent plan, but I'd kept checking the box and it had been empty. I didn't know of any other way to get to 1911, or how else to get something of Seathan's.

But Raúl—Miguel was his relative, and he bore the curse. Maybe he'd donate a little blood for the cause. A cause he didn't believe in.

Exhaling my frustration, I jammed my notebook into my bag, slid the bread into the oven, grabbed the plate—and nearly dropped it on the floor. The room swam out of focus, and, I swore by all that was holy, the house either mimicked my sigh or made one of its own. My vision cleared as soon as its song of irritation tapered off. I was still in the kitchen and I was still me, standing with the plate in my hand.

"I'm just as annoyed as you are," I said to the empty space. "God damn." I brushed through the doorway.

Grandma and I devoured the snack plate and the refill I'd made after it.

"I know you and your father are in the habit of working from sunrise to sunset, but I think that's quite enough productivity for me for one day." Grandma topped off our lemonades from the sweating pitcher. We'd killed almost the entire thing, and even though today wasn't as wickedly hot as it could be, it was warm enough.

"Want me to take you home?"

"No, your father said he'd get me this afternoon. I've got a good book I'd like to spend some more time with in the meanwhile." She took a sip. "What are you going to work on?"

I blinked. I wasn't prepared for that question. "I dunno," I stammered. "Um, I did a little research on this house's history, and I thought I'd sift through that, then go re-install the cabinet doors in the kitchen." *Dig through the hidden stairwell, research witchcraft, the usual.*

"I'm making a shrimp and scallop risotto, so come home in time for dinner. Why haven't you two just moved up here yet? It's ready enough. You're wasting time driving back and forth."

"I know. I'm starting to feel that way too. My room's done. Can I just live in it now?"

"Two little things first. That bread'll be done by now, and I'm going to need for you to find me a hammer. Do you have a hand sledge?"

"Um, no? I have a normal sledge hammer in the garage though."

"That'll do. Go get it, dear."

The house smelled like heaven, or what heaven would smell like if Martha Stewart reigned as domestic goddess.

Grandma took a deep breath and let it out slowly. "Cooking makes a house a home, and baking bread brings blessings. You should do it regularly—for health, not just for food."

"Okay." Though I'd never heard dieticians extol the virtues of a carb-based diet. "It smells nicer than a Glade Plug-in anyway. Teach me?" I followed her into the kitchen.

"Of course, dear." She used the quilted hem of her apron as an oven mitt and deposited the steaming loaf atop the range.

"For dinner tonight?"

"No. This should be eaten here. Never you mind—we'll manage."

My mouth was already watering. "I don't doubt it."

"Let's give that a minute to rest, and you won't speed it up any by staring at it. Quit dawdling and go get that mallet for me."

She was waiting for me on the stone patio when I emerged from the dark garage. "This is the part I want you to do." She handed me a railroad spike and showed me the three in her other fist. "Drive these into the ground at the corners of your property. If you and your father ever move away, pull them out."

"Okay. Do I have to do anything while I'm hammering them?"

"Try not to hit your hand."

"Well, yeah. I just thought—never mind." I headed for the most accessible corner first, where the alley met Grove, and found a patch of soil at the edge of the flagstones. I placed the tip of the spike and tapped it gently until it stood by itself. "How deep should it be?"

"You can pound it flat to the surface, if you want, but it'll be hard to find it if you need to take it out."

"Okay." I stepped back and smacked it with two solid blows, leaving the head sticking out only a few inches.

"Nice work."

I had to squeeze into an eighteen-inch space between the garage and the fence to drive the second spike, and a giant pair of blue spruces scratched the shit out of my arms for my effort. The two in the front yard were a piece of cake by comparison.

Grandma followed to supervise and nodded her approval after each one.

"Good girl. Now go put that away, and we'll have a slice of homemade bread, shall we?"

"Definitely."

A few minutes later we were in the kitchen again. Grandma inverted the pan and shook out the loaf without damaging it.

I rummaged in my bag for my lip balm and the whole thing capsized, spilling my keys, pens, and notebook onto the counter.

"What's that?" Grandma jutted her chin toward the journal, which was pretty cool looking with its hand-tooled leather cover.

"My notebook? Just where I write stuff I'm trying to remember."

"What a very antiquated technique. I approve."

I flipped the cover to some of the drawings and handed it to her. I leaned over her shoulder as she flipped the pages. An old-fashioned dress with corseting and bustle. A bird in a cherry tree. A hairpin made of wire, with a bumblebee perched at its point.

"Beautiful," she murmured.

She turned the page again, but that page was just my list of Laurel and Hazel's family members.

"Where did you get this?" she asked.

"What?"

"The Scott family tree. I don't have any of that." She turned the notebook and held it at arm's length to study the page more carefully. "My mother never talked about her family."

"Your mother was a Scott?"

"Yes." She pointed to a name at the bottom of the tree. "Right here. Laurel Anne Scott."

CHAPTER

TWENTY-NINE

I staggered backward, away from her, away from the notebook with *my own* family tree in it. And I studied Grandma's face for the thousandth time in my life, only this time I saw it. *Really* saw it.

Crescent-shaped eyes, like half moons resting sideways on high cheekbones. Laurel's were like that, but green instead of brown. Grandma's wild curls were silver, but I didn't know how I'd missed it before. If Laurel looked familiar to me, it's because she'd looked like Grandma, or Grandma looked like her, rather.

"Laurel Scott? Laurel is your mother?"

Grandma blinked as if to say, *Do not ask me to repeat myself.*

"Wait, Laurel is my great-grandmother?"

Another blink and a half nod. "Where did you get this? I'm certain your father can't know this much if I don't."

The doorbell chimed before I could answer, and we turned to the hallway. Jenny waved from the front step.

"Come on in," I called. "It's unlocked."

My father appeared on the steps behind her. "What's

with the sudden formality, Jenny? You know you're welcome to come right in at our house." He reached past and opened the door for her.

"At the old house, yeah, but it feels different here."

"Oh, good," he said. "We've turned over a new leaf of refinement and respectability."

"It's working," she said. "Oh my God, it smells heavenly in here."

"You're just in time, both of you," Grandma said. "Come have some hot bread."

I leaned back against the counter, still blinking, as Grandma tore the bread with her hands and set hunks of it in front of each of us.

"Will your beau be joining us, dear?" she asked me.

I shook my head and blinked, then registered that I've inadvertently answered her question incorrectly. "Yeah." I glanced at my watch. "He said one fifteen."

She set aside a chunk. "We'll save this bit for him."

Dad picks up his bit of bread, and Grandma swatted his hand before he could bring it to his mouth.

"I haven't blessed it yet," she said. She didn't close her eyes, just looked at us each in turn like she was continuing the conversation. "May this bread be the first of many loaves broken amid smiles and laughter of family and friends. May food never be scarce. May love abound. And may all who inhabit these walls be safe, healthy, and blessed. Let's eat."

"Amen?" I asked.

Grandma chuckled. "It isn't that kind of prayer, my dear, but you're always welcome to voice your agreement with me." She kissed my forehead.

The bread tasted as heavenly as it smelled. It collapsed into a warm goo that stuck to the roof of my mouth. I'd have been in heaven if I hadn't been so distracted. I needed to catch up with Jenny, but I was still trying to make sense of Laurel being my great-grandmother.

Laurel was my great-grandmother. Hazel was Grandma's aunt.

My great-grandmother had been in love with Miguel's great-great uncle.

Seathan was my great-great grandfather. I was related to that monster.

A piece of bread lodged too far back in my throat. Tears sprang into my eyes, and I grabbed for my water bottle.

I was Seathan's token.

"You okay?" Jenny asked.

"Uh huh." I swiped at the tears at the corners of my eyes. "Are you on your way to work?" I asked her.

"Yeah. I'm on at two."

"Do you still like it?" If I got her talking I'd have time to think some more.

"Oh my God, Kaz, I love it. I mean, I thought I'd just be doing my time answering phones, folding towels, and sweeping up hair—and I do all that—but Libby is already showing me how to mix color. I'll start shampooing soon, and then I'll be an apprentice."

The corners of my mouth twitched upward. I couldn't help it. Her enthusiasm was contagious.

The screen door creaked. "Hello?" Miguel called from the entry.

"See, Jenny?" Dad said. "Miguel has it figured out. C'mon in," he called. "We've saved you some hot bread."

Miguel crossed the kitchen to stand next to me, and for a moment I was paralyzed by the fear that he'd kiss me in front of my dad and everyone. But he didn't, and then I was a little disappointed, so I felt stupid for thinking it would have been a problem if he had. He did, however, reward me with one of his heavy-lidded half smiles, and my face warmed.

"Miguel, this is my grandma, Felicity West. Grandma, this is Miguel."

He squared his shoulders and extended his hand like a businessman, but his expression was warm, not formal. "I'm pleased to meet you, Mrs. West."

Grandma's face broke into a schoolgirl smile.

Yeah, Grandma. He had the same effect on me.

"It's a pleasure to finally meet you. Have a bite of bread."

"Thank you so much. It smells delicious."

A third of the loaf still remained. "You kids eat this, okay?" Grandma said. "Jim, are you ready? I'd like you to take me to the supermarket."

"Yeah, Mom." He leveled his gaze on me. "I'm trusting you, Kaz. You three be good." He turned to Miguel and clapped him on the shoulder. "I like you, Miguel. Don't give me reason to change that."

Miguel didn't bat an eyelash. "Of course not, sir." He took an enormous bite from his slice of the bread.

I covered my face with my hand.

Jenny smiled, enjoying the show.

"God, my dad is so embarrassing sometimes," I said after the screen door clattered shut behind them.

"You have absolutely nothing to complain about," Jenny said. "My father would never let me hang out, unsupervised, with a boy. Ever. Never mind that I've not given him any reason to distrust me."

"It's not you he distrusts," Miguel said. "It's the boys."

"That's an erroneous extrapolation of Puritanical misogynistic beliefs. Females are just as sexual as males. It's patriarchal societal expectations that force women to shelve our wants and needs as though they should matter less to us than the interests of others."

I buttered another chunk of bread and took a bite before saying, "Want to tell us how you really feel?"

"Enough of that. I'm here for the news." She hoisted herself up and perched on the kitchen counter. "You're totally distracted, so I know something's up. What's the latest with Hazel and Laurel?"

My jaw dropped, and I blinked twice.

Miguel turned to me. "Who are Hazel and Laurel?"

Shit.

I glanced to Miguel and back to Jenny.

She didn't miss it. She didn't let it go either. "I thought you were going to tell him. How have you not told him?"

Miguel raised his brows and turned to me expectantly. Not mad, curious.

"I didn't know how to bring it up."

"It's as much his story as yours—more even. It's his family."

"Actually, that is the news." I picked a bread crumb from the counter and popped it in my mouth. "It's my family too. That's what I just found out. God, I'm so confused."

Miguel turned to Jenny and repeated his question. "Who are Hazel and Laurel?"

"Laurel is your great-great uncle's girlfriend," she said.

"Was," he corrected.

"Yeah, only it's been seeming more like the present," she said.

He furrowed his brow and turned to me, waiting for more.

I sucked air through my teeth. "I just found out Laurel is my great grandmother."

"No effin' way!" Jenny exclaimed. "Raúl was dating your great-grandma, and now, generations later, you two wind up together? That's too weird. What if it's some crazy multi-generational pheromone alignment?"

"Are you two planning on filling me in at some point?" Miguel interjected.

Jenny cocked her head and looked meaningfully at me.

"Let's go sit down. This is going to take a while," I said. I took his hand, probably more to see if he'd pull it away. I was feeling a bit miffed at Jenny for forcing the issue.

She grabbed three sodas from the fridge and followed us to the entryway.

"So you know that box I found in the stairway?" I began.

"Yeah."

"Well, it had a hairpin in it. When I touched it, I passed out and saw things. Stuff about your family and mine."

His brows knit together and he nodded. I couldn't read his expression.

"Raúl was dating Laurel, but her dad put a stop to it when he found out. He was racist."

"Star-crossed lovers," Jenny said.

"They tried to run away together, but something happened and Raúl was hurt."

"What happened to your great-grandmother?" he asked.

"I don't know. I haven't seen anything else about her. She must have wound up in California at some point because that's where my grandma was born."

"Okay. That's all very interesting, but it doesn't explain why you're upset."

I wrung my hands in my lap. "Okay, so you know that journal page I showed you? The one 'Uela freaked out about?"

"Yeah." He looked guarded.

"I got that from the box, but those things all disappear after I touch them. I'm not imagining it. You saw the pictures yourself."

"Okay." His smile was totally gone, but he waited for me to continue.

"It was a hex. I think Raúl's mom did that."

Jenny gasped. "Oh my God. Now I see why you didn't tell him. Your grandfather is the reason—"

"I didn't tell him because I didn't know how to explain where I got the information. I didn't know Seathan was my great-great grandfather until today. Grandma just told me. But, yeah, my great-great grandfather was an asshole. He's the reason your family lost the house."

"'Uela's mother sold the house when her husband committed suicide," Miguel said.

"Who, Horacio?" I asked. "Oh my God, I didn't know he killed himself." I covered my face with my hands and left them there as I continued. "Seathan and Horacio were in the solarum industry together, before anyone knew what radiation poisoning was." I uncovered my face and grabbed Miguel's hands. "Horacio was sick, his son died unexpectedly, and his business collapsed. Seathan cashed out and left Horacio holding the loans when the company folded."

Miguel's gaze shifted back and forth from one of my eyes to the other, and the corners of his mouth twitched up in an amused expression. "Kaz, do you think I'm going to hold it against you that some ancestor of yours was an asshole to some ancestor of mine?" His smile disappeared for a second. "Oh shit, we're not related, are we?"

I stopped and thought for a minute. "No, we couldn't be. My grandma wasn't born until 1933. Raúl died in 1911." I squinted while I counted off on my fingers. "Wow, she was, like, thirty-nine or something before she had a kid."

"Well, that's a relief," Miguel said, leaned in and softly bit my lower lip.

"Hey, guys, I'm still right here," Jenny said in a monotone.

"Oh yeah. Don't you have someplace you need to be?" Miguel asked.

"Nope. Not for another half hour, I don't."

"Darn," he said.

"Do you think I'm crazy?" I asked, my face still inches from Miguel's.

"How could I think you're crazy? I've seen the pictures."

"But you don't buy into 'Uela's mysticism."

"I never said that. I don't want to believe 'Uela's mysticism. If she had her way I'd be locked safely in my room until I'm forty. Still, stuff happens all the time that I can't explain."

"Do you believe in the curse?" Jenny asked bluntly.

He pulled away from me to include her more. "No. I don't."

I blinked and shook my head. "Then how do you explain these near-misses? The car crash? The collapsed shelves?"

"Coincidence?" he asked. "I don't think the universe has it out for me."

I sat back and exhaled. I didn't know what to say.

Jenny shook her head. "You know what? You two have some more talking to do, and it might score me brownie points if I show up to work early."

"You don't have to go, Jenny. Really. We like having you here," I said.

"Nope. You need to get this worked out," she said. "Do you know what today is?"

"Thursday?"

"Yeah," she said. "Thursday, June 20. Summer solstice."

"Oh."

"So you should talk to 'Uela about reversing the curse tonight."

THIRTY

09:30PM ME: Meet me at the house?
09:30PM Miguel: Okay. 10?
09:31PM ME: Yeah.

I grabbed my shoes and slipped silently down the hall past Dad's door and past Grandma's. I'd never snuck out before, but I'd been thinking about it all evening. The front door was too loud, so I eased the sliding glass door open and cringed when the weather stripping made a sucking sound.

I closed it behind me, but there was no way to lock it from this side. I guessed it'd just be easier to get back in then.

I jammed my feet into my boots and left the laces wrapped loosely at the ankle, which made it harder to hop the gate, but the thing squeaked too loudly to risk opening it.

My faithful truck was parked at the curb. The engine was loud and so distinctive, Dad would catch me the moment I turned the key. I unlocked the door and slid into the driver's seat. Popping it into neutral, I cranked the wheel and pushed on the doorframe. It was heavy at first, but the street sloped downhill from the house, so I jumped in and rode with it until I was several houses away. Then I snapped my seatbelt, closed my door properly, and fired up the engine.

There was almost no traffic, so I arrived ten minutes earlier than I'd expected. Miguel was already on the porch step, leaning on the support. He looked so hot in his soccer shorts. If his windbreaker didn't have the junior league logo on it, he would pass for a pro athlete.

"Hey, beautiful." He was at my door before I unhooked my seatbelt.

"Hey, handsome." I turned sideways in the seat, but he was blocking the doorway. I wrapped my arms around his neck and lifted my chin.

His lips met mine, and he pulled me to him, pressing our bodies together.

Cinnamon gum.

Ropy muscle.

I could have stayed right there all night long. I was tempted to. I'd not been looking forward to this task—I still didn't know what I was doing.

Miguel pulled away and tapped the brass goggles I was wearing as a headband. "These are dope. They're perfect on you."

"Thanks," I grabbed my bag and let him lead me from the truck. "What do you know about burning smudges?"

"Plenty. I've never actually done it, but I've seen 'Uela do it a thousand times."

I unlocked the front door.

"Don't you have candles?" Miguel asked when I flipped the light switch.

"Yeah. There are some in the sideboard, actually."

"You're not supposed to use electricity while you're casting."

"I didn't know that. Okay. I thought you didn't believe in this stuff?"

"I don't believe in vampires either, but I know you're supposed to fight them with garlic. You can be aware of a process without buying into it."

"I guess I thought you had changed your mind. You seemed more open-minded about it earlier. Like you believed me."

We were in the living room under the ornate ceiling. His angular features were illuminated by the hall light.

"I believe *you*," he said. "I have no doubt that you experienced something out of the ordinary, and that you know things as a result that you wouldn't have known otherwise. I think weird stuff is real. I think protective dances are fake. But I love you, so I'm here because you want me to be."

"You love me?"

"Of course I love you."

"You've known me for less than a week."

"Okay, so maybe I'm just infatuated. My point is, I'm here because I like you. Kind of a lot."

"Does your mom know where you are?"

"No, but 'Uela does." He held up his wrist. "She restrung my *mal de ojo*."

I tried to explain my plan and Miguel nodded in understanding, making me wonder if it made more sense to him than it did to me.

"You can't make a smudge out of this." Miguel pulled a leaf from the spurge and rolled it between his fingers. "It's still green. It won't burn."

I slapped my palm to my forehead. "I should've dried it

in the oven this afternoon. Dammit. Now what am I going to do?"

"I've seen 'Uela throw fresh herbs directly into the fire. Or maybe, since your sage is dried, we can make a stick with that on the outside and the living leaves in the center. The dry herbs will help these burn. We could try that."

"*We* nothing, Miguel. I'm glad you're here to talk me through this—I need your expertise—but I don't want you to do the cast. 'Uela thinks the spell backfired in the first place because the *curanderos* are forbidden to do black magic. It could be a bloodline thing. I don't want to take chances."

"But you need my blood to cast?"

"Yeah. Stop trying to make sense of it."

Miguel carried my carton of supplies to the basement.

I pulled a hurricane lantern from the shelf. There was fuel—kerosene?—in the reservoir already. "Does this stuff go bad?" I asked and swirled the liquid to aerate it some.

"I don't think so. Petroleum is made of sixty-five million-year-old dinosaur guts, so I don't see it going bad in a person's lifetime. Do you have a lighter?"

"Matches."

He adjusted the wick and passed it to me with a nod. I struck the match and the room blazed with light.

"Perfect." He replaced the glass chimney and pulled two more lanterns down from the shelf. He set them in front of me. "Three is an auspicious number. Here—you adjust it. You only need about an eighth of an inch of wick. And swirling the oil probably wasn't a terrible idea."

I lit them as directed. "How do you know so much about lanterns?"

"There's not much to know about them—they're pretty simple. But I work in a hardware store, and these are actually still pretty popular to have on hand for blizzards, tornado season, or just for preppers who obsess about surviving a zombie apocalypse."

"Or witches who avoid electricity—"

"On that note, I'll take this and go turn off the lights upstairs. Do you want me to take your cell phone up there? I'm just going to leave mine on the bench by the door."

I handed it off and laid the supplies out in order on the table.

The pot-bellied stove in the corner of the basement was clean inside, and it only at that moment occurred to me that it might not function. What if the chimney was blocked, or had been capped?

Miguel must have had the same thought. He pulled a handle inside the stove and opened the flue, then lit a twist of newspaper and held it at the door of the stove. The curl of smoke caught in the draft and wafted into the stove and up the chimney. It worked.

"Let's just hope the chimney isn't full of leaves and squirrel carcasses, or some other flammable crap," I said.

I built a small fire with newspapers and scrap two-by-fours.

"You know you're not really supposed to use prepared lumber as firewood, right?" he said.

"It's pine. Don't be nit-picky."

Miguel looked over my scrawled recipe. "The salt and dirt should probably go last—they'll deaden the fire."

"I'm pretty sure the bandages were last the first time."

"Then be careful not to put too much in."

Miguel showed me how to lay out the sage. I made a line of juniper and spurge up the center, then layered more dried sage over it. I bound it off with natural jute twine I'd found in the garage. It wasn't as pretty as the ones I saw on YouTube, but Miguel said it would work.

Once the blaze had taken, I used it to light my smudge wand.

He sat on a stack of cinderblocks. "While you're saging, concentrate on your breathing and visualize the smoke doing its job—purifying and—what else is it supposed to do?"

I glanced at the scrawl. "Um, spiritual safety?"

"And the juniper?"

"To open the eyes."

"Okay then. Try to connect it to your breathing. With each inhale, think about it purifying you, and imagine yourself exhaling a shield of safety. And with each cycle, visualize your sight becoming clearer."

"Okay." I took a deep breath, and coughed it out. The smudge smelled exactly like the one Raúl's mother used. And, of course, it should have. But I hadn't considered how distressing that would be.

I held it well away from my face and took several deep calming breaths, then set to it.

Inhaled. *Purify.* Exhaled. *Protect.*

I smudged the circle in which I'd be working, then circumnavigated the room. I paid special attention to the two windows, the old coal chute, and directed the cleansing smoke into each corner, including the stairwell. Then I smudged the circle one more time.

Inhaled—purify. Exhaled—protect.

The miners' bane was supposed to activate my intention. It may have actually worked, because my will was cemented. I could do this.

"Is that good enough, do you think?"

"Probably. Are you just going to toss it into the fire?"

"I guess so."

The fire leapt when I threw the smoking stick onto it—like the sap had been made of gasoline. I was caught so off guard, I leaned back from the hot blue-green fingers and forgot I was supposed to be concentrating.

Clear vision. Intention.

Miguel whispered from behind me. "You have to do the rest on your own."

I whipped around and faced him. "You're not leaving, are you?"

"No." He pulled my goggles from my head, adjusted them, and put them back on over my eyes.

I turned back to my carton of supplies and the fire. I had to pause to tighten the knot on my bracelet, which had worked itself loose. I hadn't known how to make the same knot 'Uela had used and mine kept coming undone. I fished out the plastic bag of dirt and cast a handful of it onto the flames. They died back significantly.

Next, the salt, which deadened the flames some more.

I was not looking forward to this next part, but I'd planned for it as best as I could. The two sharpest knives from our kitchen, sterilized with rubbing alcohol and stored in plastic, two packets of cotton gauze, and two fat Band-Aids.

I set one of each on the table. One gauze, I gave to Miguel.

He gave me his left hand.

"I'm sorry," I whispered.

I squeezed the middle finger on his hand to deaden the sensation, then, trying not to belabor it, slid the blade across the skin.

Bright red blood immediately filled the gash I'd made, and he pressed the gauze to it.

I turned to the other supplies and did the same to my own left hand.

I caught my blood, and when it stopped I cast the gauze pad into the flames.

The fire didn't seem to notice.

I shrugged, grabbed Miguel's bloody gauze strip and realized too late as I cast it into the fire that my bracelet had come undone again. It, with the milagro and my little brass gear, went into the fire with the bloody cotton. I almost didn't register the white explosion it fired back to me.

Lightning.

THIRTY-ONE

I knew where I was by the smell of it. 1911. And there was another aroma too. Wintertime chimneys.

Brightness seared my eyes the moment I dared to peek, but in an instant I was wide awake.

Fire. Above me. All around me.

I jumped to my feet before my mind fully registered what I was doing.

Stay low. I dropped into a crouch, skirts billowing around me.

Raúl lay on the concrete by my knee. Unconscious.

Raúl was dead.

I pressed my fingertips into his neck and found a pulse. He wasn't dead.

Raúl is dead, my mind insisted.

No, he clearly was not. But if we didn't get out of here, we both would be.

The fire roared above us and on three sides—the stone wall at my back the only surface not aflame. The floorboards above us bubbled from the heat.

If the fire and smoke didn't kill us, a collapsing house would.

Something heavy creaked and crashed about twenty feet away, sending up a plume of smoke and debris. I shielded Raúl with my arms, but the cloud of dust was held away from us by an invisible barrier.

I extended a shaking hand to where the smoke curled away from us and found the edge. It was like sticking my fingertips in a furnace.

I pulled back and cowered beside Raúl's form.

There, amid the crackling of the flames and my gasping breath, the incessant clanging of a bell.

Hazel! my head screamed. *Hazel!*

A fire fighter stood at the foot of the stairs. He shielded his eyes, looked right past me, and turned away.

He couldn't see me.

"Help!" I opened my mouth to yell, but the word didn't come out. My lips made the shape, but in this nightmare, I couldn't utter a sound.

Alone.

Get up, Hazel. Get out.

The voice took a shape in the dancing flames. Laurel stood, unburnt, on the flaming steps. *You have to save yourself.*

I shook Raúl.

Raúl is dead. You have to save yourself.

He was not dead. He was breathing.

You have to save yourself.

I cast a pleading look her way, but the stairs were empty.

I wiped at my eyes and found 'Uela's *mal de ojo* charm still tied to my wrist. But I was in Hazel's clothes.

I jammed a hand in my pocket. Instead of the CommuniClock I pulled out a tiny vial. The one 'Uela gave me yesterday. *Copal.*

I was supposed to burn it, right?

Crazy things happened in this dream. Firemen couldn't see me. I couldn't talk. I sat in a smoke-free-fire-free bubble, and Laurel screamed in my head.

Maybe I was strong.

Maybe I couldn't get burned.

Maybe it didn't matter if I was dreaming anyway.

I uncapped the vial and flung the contents into the flames. The drops hit the wall of smoke and burst into white puffs. I took three deep breaths, then returned to Raúl.

I grabbed him by his armpits and raised him to a sitting position, bracing him that way with my knee to his back.

Was I really going to carry this guy while I was wearing a skirt and a corset? Eff this.

But I tried. I straddled his legs and hoisted him to a stand. I had to shove my shoulder into his gut, pinning him against the rock wall, and he just kind of crumpled against my shoulders, so I grabbed his arm and his leg and hoisted him with my shoulders.

He was so flipping heavy.

The smoke and heat at the edge of the bubble formed a gelatinous barrier.

I leaned back into it and took three deep breaths, and pushed out into the heat.

Raúl must have weighed at least as much as I did, but it was easier to move.

Gone were the skirts and layers. I was me. Work boots. Cutoff shorts. Flannel shirt. Goggles.

I hauled us to the stairs.

I was definitely not immune to fire.

Flames licked my calves, but I pushed through as fast as I could. Burns could heal. I couldn't fix dead.

The second-to-top step collapsed under our weight and I cracked my knee against the tread above it.

I cried out and heard nothing but roaring flames.

It must have made a sound, because a fire fighter appeared in the opening, and his viselike grip bit into my arm.

I sucked in a breath, but it was all smoke that burned my throat. Raúl's weight disappeared from my shoulders, and my palms sank into the bubbling linoleum. My eyes widened in horror, and my body reacted. My burnt hands and leg jerked involuntarily back in to my core, leaving me balancing on the one leg with any purchase.

I vaulted myself across the floor, not registering setting my feet at all, but I must have because I was there to see the fire fighter deposit Raúl on the flagstones and turn.

His eyes widened as though he were surprised to see me there. "Is there anyone else in the house?" he yelled around his mask.

I nodded my head. Then I shook it. "I don't think so."

A glance behind me showed flames reaching out the back door of the house and an arc of spray from a fire hose.

And I was out.

THIRTY-TWO

ad and Grandma's voices drifted around me.

"I dreamt she was in trouble."

"I thought you didn't remember your dreams."

"I don't. This one woke me up."

My chest rose and fell in a forced rhythm, keeping time with a beep beside my bed.

Another voice. "She's very fortunate. Patients in her situation usually have to be treated for carbon monoxide poisoning and extensive burns, but her levels are almost normal."

I wanted to cough, but I didn't have control over my breath—the machine did.

"And Miguel?" Dad asked.

I didn't hear the answer.

The next time I came to, I was alone.

This time my mind was less foggy. Light filtered through my lashes. I still had a mask over my nose and mouth, but my chest wasn't being forced into a prescribed breathing pattern. I took a deep breath.

And my eyelids sagged shut again.

When my eyes snapped open, I was indescribably thirsty.

"Water?" I croaked. I had tubes in my nose, but the mask was gone.

At once Dad and Grandma were at my side.

"I'll tell the nurse," Grandma said.

"Water," I tried to say again.

Dad tilted a little cup to my mouth.

I drained it, then coughed.

He put his hand to my head to soothe me. "We've been awfully worried about you, little girl. The doctors say you're going to be okay. How do you feel?"

"Hands hurt."

"Yeah, I'd guess so. Those are going to be bandaged for a while, but I'd expect they probably hurt. You burned them pretty badly."

The fire. Melted linoleum. Raúl.

"Where is—Raúl?" *No, that didn't even make sense. Raúl was in 1911.*

"Who?" Dad asked.

"Carried. Fire. Raúl." I was so tired. Talking made me sleepy.

"You carried Miguel. He's okay."

He was okay.

I'd been out of the hospital for a week. Miguel and I sat on the retaining wall across from the house and watched construction workers carry two-by-fours into the house.

The construction fence was back.

It was a total gut of the kitchen, and the flooring joists had to be replaced or sistered with new wood. The pros kept commenting on how odd it was that the rest of the house was almost unaffected—not even by smoke. Almost like it'd had a shield.

Or a blessing.

Miguel said, "The firemen said you carried me out like a boss."

"I barely remember it," I said.

"Neither one of us would've been in that situation if you hadn't had to protect me."

"The curse?"

"The curse."

"D'you believe in it now?"

"I don't think that was a normal fire. Do you?"

"Do you think it worked?"

"Ten days and no close calls with death."

"What's 'Uela say?"

"I don't know. I haven't asked her directly. She just keeps smiling and hugging me."

"Sounds like a good sign."

"Yeah." He ran a finger along an un-bandaged patch of my arm, and I shivered.

"I sure wouldn't mind a few more good signs," I said.

THIRTY-THREE

"What do you think about this for above the fireplace?" Dad pulled a gilded floral-edged mirror from the back of my truck. "The antique store on Tejon had it on the sidewalk."

"I love that." I ran my thumb along the cracked edge of the frame.

"Do you want to refinish it?" Miguel asked.

"Maybe at some point, but let's just get something up there. It's too boring and blank as it is."

Miguel helped me carry it into the living room, where we eased the mirror onto the sofa. It was really heavy.

I buffed a blemish from the glass with my sleeve, and the image shifted. In the reflection, my short post-fire layered hair was longer—in a ponytail—and I was wearing a new flannel shirt. Etched on the picture window behind me were the words—MONTAÑO AND WEST. URBAN ARCHITECTURE AND RENOVATION.

I leaned to the side to catch a glimpse of Miguel in the mirror, but the image shifted back, and there we were, just like before. The giant window behind me was bare, but for a shiny new set of blinds.

Miguel turned around and caught my odd expression. "What's up?"

I opened my mouth to tell him what I saw, but then closed it and smiled. "Three weeks until you start at CU, huh?"

"Yeah. I'm really lucky that STEM scholarship applied to architectural studies."

"I saw that they have a degree in construction engineering and management. I keep thinking I'd like to be a contractor." I snapped my toolbelt around my waist.

"We could go into business together."

"That's exactly what I was thinking."

Miguel handed me the screwdriver, which I dropped into its spot in my pouch. He moved in and kissed me, first high on my cheekbone and again, longer, on my lips.

We leaned against the fireplace wall for balance in our contented delirium. A tremor sighed through the wall behind me—the bricks exhaling a quivering breath. It felt like relief.

ACKNOWLEDGMENTS

It takes a village to write a debut novel. My village is made up of the brilliant and magical WPF faculty and students of Seton Hill University, where I found my people and overheard the most fascinating elevator conversations concerning the factors that affect corpse decomposition in freshwater streams. Thank you for normalizing weirdness.

Thanks particularly to the Trifecta of Cat Herd—Melanie Bates and Christopher M. Tantillo—as well as Shelley Adina and Heidi Ruby Miller, all of whom read this manuscript more times than anyone should have to. To my mom, Elaine Wilcox, *tusen takk* for the limitless love and support; you may be my biggest fan, and I return that sentiment in kind. Thank you also, beta readers and friends, for your guidance and encouragement in writing my first book. *Takk skal du ha.*

ABOUT THE AUTHOR

Effie Rose lives with her sons and her dog in an old house oddly similar to Kaz's. She has an MFA in Writing Popular Fiction from Seton Hill University. When she's not writing, she moonlights as a paralegal, plays in her garden, and fixes her own crumbling residence.